Honey for the Devil

In order to keep the secret of her past, Sally never invites anyone to the isolated cottage in Cornwall where she lives with her grandmother.

Her greatest pleasure is acting in the local theatre, and she is flattered by the attentions of suave Nicholas Dewer – until she discovers that he is boss of the construction company planning to demolish the theatre. Sally is leading the campaign to save it and she is determined to fight every step of the way.

Nick declares he always gets what he wants, and when he starts turning her life upside own, she realizes that what he wants is her!

HONEY FOR THE DEVIL

RAINBOW ROMANCE

JAN ROBINS

ROBERT HALE · LONDON

© Jan Robins 1992
First published in Great Britain 1992

ISBN 0 7090 4888 2

Robert Hale Limited
Clerkenwell House
Clerkenwell Green
London EC1R 0HT

Printed and bound by Interprint Ltd.,
Valletta, Malta.

One

He was there again.

Only now, as she bowed her golden head to acknow-ledge the applause, would Sally admit to herself that she had been aware of him from the very beginning. For the past couple of hours she had been Juliet, painfully and fatally in love with Romeo. Now the play had ended and the audience were clapping their approval.

No, not all of them. That dark man in the centre of the front row wasn't clapping. His hands were clasped in the usual position, but they weren't moving. In all that enthu-siastic crowd, he alone was perfectly still, his eyes fixed on her.

Sally touched her tongue to her lips. There was some-thing sinister in his intense gaze. Who was he? Last night he sat in the same seat, watching the same play, and, like last night, he was wearing a dinner-jacket. That alone would have set him apart from the regular audience. This wasn't Drury Lane! It was an amateur dramatic society performing in a small Cornish market town. The locals never dressed formally to come to The Duke's Theatre.

But the dark stranger was immaculate, and he had come twice.

There was a flurry of excitement on stage. Sally tore her gaze away from him and her blue eyes widened in amaze-ment as an enormous bouquet of red roses was thrust into her hands.

She gazed at it in astonishment. They rarely gave

bouquets at The Duke's. It was a sort of unwritten rule not to waste money, every penny was needed for the fighting fund to keep the theatre from closure. This bouquet must have cost a small fortune.

As she breathed the heady perfume of the roses, Sally felt that this was a sign. And she knew who had sent it. She lifted her radiant face to the audience, then gave a special smile to the man in the front row.

He bowed his dark head very slightly in acknowledgement. He must be someone from the theatrical world who had come to save their theatre from demolition, the benefactor they had all been hoping for. Her heart almost bursting with happiness, she bowed once more to the audience.

Suddenly the curtain came down. Everyone on stage glanced anxiously at the flies to see if the cord had snapped, or the props man had made a mistake, but the stage manager signalled that he was giving them another curtain call.

Anita, the girl who played the nurse, leaned over to Sally and whispered, "Handsome devil, isn't he?"

Sally felt a shiver run down her spine. That described the stranger exactly. He was certainly handsome, but there was more than a hint of the Devil in his classic features and the arrogant lift of his head.

Applause thundered as the curtain rose again. Sally kept her eyes resolutely away from the front row, gazing over their heads to the people at the back.

Jake Treherne, the male lead, reached for her hand, and Romeo and Juliet took a bow together. This was Saturday, their last night, and they were going to make the most of it.

At last, the curtain came down.

Jake drew Sally towards him and kissed her resoundingly on the cheek. "You were great."

"You too," she whispered and glanced around. "I think we were all great."

Anita laughed softly. "It's always the way. By the last night we've really got it all together. Now we've got to forget it all and start learning our lines for the next one."

As they made their way off stage, Jake said, "The Green Room everyone. We've got the press, remember."

"Sounds grand," Anita murmured, following Sally into the room at the side of the stage. "It'll be Larry from the *Gazette*."

Sally smiled. "It's all publicity, and we need as much as we can get."

The room was fairly small but they all squeezed in, the principals and the extras, many of whom had been borrowed from the Operatic Society. With the threat of demolition hanging over them, all the societies were pulling together to make maximum use of the theatre to show that the town really needed it. *Romeo and Juliet* was the most ambitious play the Dramatic Society had ever staged and they had called on all the help they could muster. Next week, some of them would be playing extras in the Operatic Society's production of *Carmen*.

Sally found herself thrust into the space in the centre of the room with the *Gazette* reporter bearing down on her. She glanced around. Where was Jake?

"Romeo, Romeo. Wherefore art thou Romeo?"

Jake emerged beside her. "A rose by any other name –"

"Hey," she laughed. "You're pinching my line."

"I'll pinch one of your roses." He pulled one from the bouquet and threaded its stem in the lacings of his leather jerkin.

"A red rose for love," he murmured, lifting her hand

and kissing it extravagantly.

"Once a ham, always a ham," Anita muttered as a camera flashed.

The *Gazette* reporter held his pencil poised over his notebook. "Is there a romance in the air?"

Jake gave him a broad grin. "Of course. We're passionately in love, aren't we, Sally?"

"Sure," she agreed. "We're all passionately in love – with this theatre. It's our theatre. It belongs to the town, to the people. We won't let it be pulled down."

A fresh-faced young man, with a microphone in one hand and a tape-recorder hitched over his shoulder, forced his way through the throng. He came over to Sally and identified himself as a reporter for the local radio station.

"Miss Penrose, I believe you're leading the campaign against the proposed development scheme. Would you be prepared to tell our listeners why?"

"Willingly." Sally glanced at Jake, who was their official spokesman, and he nodded for her to go ahead.

The reporter held the microphone in front of her. "As soon as I switch on, I'd like you to give your name. Then I'll ask you the question, and you reply. OK?"

"Just give me a few seconds to gather my thoughts." .

The room had gone very quiet, everyone seemed to be holding their breath, including Sally. She knew she had to put their case clearly and persuasively. She also knew that everyone was with her. As she glanced around to gather strength from their support, she caught sight of the man in the dinner-jacket. He was standing in the corner as though trying to merge into the background.

As if that was possible!

He was the sort of man who would stand out in any crowd, especially here. The Cornish are naturally of short stature and he was a head taller than anyone else in the room.

His dark eyes were fixed on her and their intensity drove every thought from her head. Almost as though he had cast a spell on her, the room seemed to dissolve and she was aware only of him.

From a long way off, she heard the reporter ask, "Ready?"

Sally blinked and gave herself a mental shake as the room came back into focus. She must forget the man. Or, better still, try to put their case convincingly to him.

She smiled confidently. "OK."

The reporter pressed the switch and she began. "I am Sally Penrose, a member of the thriving Duke's Theatre Dramatic Society. We have been performing *Romeo and Juliet* by William Shakespeare to capacity audiences for the past fortnight." No need to admit that it was only three nights a week.

The reporter said, "I understand there are plans to demolish the theatre to make way for a commercial development."

Her blue eyes flashed with anger. "That's right. Some money-grubbing developer wants to tear it down. To build a supermarket, of all things!"

Her voice rose dramatically. "This lovely old building has been standing here for two-hundred years. Two centuries of history to be bulldozed for short-term commercial gain. The Duke's Theatre is the hub of our cultural activity, the very heart of our community. If it is destroyed, the town will bleed to death!"

She paused for effect, then added firmly, "We cannot let that happen."

There were cries of, "Never!" "We'll fight!" "They can't do it!"

Sally glanced at the stranger. He was still watching her, but now there was a cynical lift to his fine dark eyebrows, making him look even more satanical. He obviously wasn't impressed by her words. Perhaps she was wrong about him. He may not be on their side.

There were plenty of arguments she could put forward – and did, on many occasions – but it wasn't her place to say any more now. This was a joint effort and it was Jake's turn next. He had briefed them all beforehand, sharing out the objections so that everyone would have something to say without too much repetition.

As the reporters interviewed each of the principal actors, the extras and bit-part players began to drift away to the dressing-rooms to change, and the Green Room gradually emptied.

When the reporters eventually left, the dark stranger came over to Sally.

"Miss Penrose, I was very impressed this evening."

He spoke softly but she knew instinctively that he was a businessman, not an actor, and he was not from the Westcountry. She smiled tentatively up into his eyes, which were so dark brown as to be almost black.

"Thank you." She lightly touched one of the roses in the bouquet she was holding. "Thank you for the flowers. It was most generous of you."

"A small token of my appreciation."

His gaze moved slowly over her and she flushed. She was wearing the white lace-trimmed gown in which Juliet had been entombed. It was very modest – but she had made it out of a nightdress!

"May I speak with you privately?" he asked.

Sally glanced around. There were a dozen or so people in the room. Jake and Anita were standing quite close and she was sure everyone was listening. But what could he have to say to her that he didn't want anyone to hear?

"I'm afraid we don't have the facilities. The dressing-rooms are communal." She waved a hand towards the door. "If you'd like to step out onto the stage...."

His eyebrows went up. "You call that private?"

She shrugged. "The audience have gone. There's nobody in the auditorium."

"And if there is, they'll hear the merest whisper spoken on the stage."

Sally smiled. "The acoustics are terrific, aren't they? It's a marvellous theatre to play in." She added eagerly, "You can see now why we must save it."

His eyes narrowed a fraction. "We can't talk here. Will you have supper with me?"

"Supper," she stammered. She knew better than to accept an invitation from a stranger, no matter how immaculate. "But I don't know who you are."

"My fault." He took a card from his inside pocket and handed it to her.

Sally glanced down at his name and her eyes widened with disbelief. The legends of Dartmoor flitted through her brain. He couldn't be! Nicholas Dewer! The Devil himself!

Black hair, black eyes, black suit, black heart....

She took a deep breath. They were only stories, she told herself. He couldn't really be the Devil.

There was a London address, St John's Wood. And a string of qualifications after his name. They didn't mean a thing to her but they included a lot of A's so they must be something to do with accountancy. He was a financier who was going to save the theatre. Perhaps he didn't want publicity, that's why he had kept in the background while the reporters were here.

She swallowed. "Mr – er – Dewer, I...."

He cut in suavely, "I'm staying at a local hotel. The landlord will vouch for me."

There were two good hotels in the town. If he said The Black Dog then she would know he was the Devil.

Almost as though reading her thoughts, he said, "The White Hart. It's just along the road."

"I know where it is." She glanced down at her costume. What on earth could she wear? She had come in jeans and a sweater, hardly suitable for The White Hart. Never mind, she would think of something. She wasn't going to pass up a chance like this. The theatre was all. She must do what she could to save it – even if that meant supper with the Devil himself.

Anita threw her a glance, then tactfully urged the others out of the room, leaving Sally alone with the stranger.

She raised her head to find his dark eyes upon her.

He took her hand. "You'll have supper with me?"

"Thank you, Mr – er – Dewer." She rubbed her fingertip on the greasepaint on her cheek. "I'll need about five minutes to clean this off."

He flicked a glance round the deserted room. "I'll wait in the foyer."

Before she could guess his intention, he lifted her hand to his lips. There was nothing amateurish or showy in his action as he lightly kissed the backs of her fingers, then turned her hand over to kiss her palm.

Sally had had her hand kissed many times, always by actors, but never like this. Her pulse began to race as she felt the warmth of his lips on her palm, his breath fanning her skin.

He touched his lips to the pulse-point on her wrist and looked up at her. There was such appeal in that upwards gaze and her heart turned over.

"Five minutes," he said softly, then dropped her hand and walked away.

Sally stood staring after him in bewilderment. Who was

he, this stranger from London? No man had ever affected her like this before. And he had only kissed her hand! She had better keep a safe distance from him this evening.

Five minutes, he had said. She turned and hurried to the dressing-room.

All the other women had gone, leaving only Anita standing before the mirror. She didn't look much like the aged nurse now she had taken off the cap which had covered her curly black hair and was busily wiping the greasepaint wrinkles off her face.

She pushed the jar of cream along to Sally.

"Wow, he's gorgeous. You've made a conquest there. Who is he?"

Sally slipped out of her dress and began applying cream liberally to her face. "His name's Nicholas Dewer."

Anita was an incomer, she hadn't been brought up on Westcountry folklore like Sally. The name meant nothing to her.

"Yes, but who is he? I mean, what does he want? Apart from the obvious, of course."

Sally frowned. "I don't know what you mean."

"Don't you, Miss Innocence?" Anita was only three years older than Sally's nineteen, but light-years older in experience. "Well, you can't wear your old jeans to The White Hart."

"I know." Sally wiped the cream off her face. "I've never been there. Do you think my Act 1 dress will be all right?"

Anita laughed. "Perfect. It makes you look about fourteen. That should keep the wolf at bay."

Fourteen was an age of maturity in old Verona, Sally thought as she put on the dress. Of gentian-blue, it was low-cut with a full skirt reaching to mid-calf, and fitted her slim figure to perfection.

Anita looked her over. "It's cold out. Borrow my shawl."

"Thanks."

Sally applied a trace of normal make-up to the delicate bone-structure of her heart-shaped face, a hint of gloss to her soft lips, then brushed out her long blonde hair that fell half-way down her back, emphasising her elfin beauty.

When she had stowed her things into her tote-bag, she reached for her bouquet, teased it apart and offered half to Anita.

"It's not fair that I should have so many flowers when nobody else gets any. You have these."

Anita smiled in delight. "They're lovely. But what's your beau going to say?"

He wasn't a beau! But there was no point in saying that to Anita.

"He won't know. I'll drop these in my car before I meet him." She glanced hastily around. "We'd better move. Joe'll be round to lock up in a minute."

The two girls hurried down the stairs to the stage door and out to the carpark at the back of the theatre.

"Good luck!" Anita called as she disappeared into the darkness.

Sally put her tote-bag and the flowers into her car, then nipped back up the stairs and through the corridor to the foyer.

Nicholas Dewer stood, tall and powerful, with his back to her, gazing through the glass doors at the deserted street outside. Feet slightly apart, his hands clasped behind him, his head erect, there was confidence in every line. A man apart, Sally thought; he would always go his own way.

The door squeaked as it began to close behind her. Nicholas Dewer swung round sharply, but stopped when he saw her. "Ah, it's you, Sally. Exactly on time too."

She was surprised by his use of her first name. "I try to

be punctual," she said softly. "One learns to change quickly in the theatre."

His gaze moved slowly over her from head to toe, his mouth curving in a smile. Then he pulled open the door to the street. "Supper awaits."

As she passed in front of him, Sally was disconcerted to see that the white handkerchief in his breast pocket was on a level with her eyes. Admittedly she was wearing the ballerina slippers she wore on stage, but she was so much shorter he must look upon her as a child.

Yet there was nothing paternal in the way he tucked her hand in his arm as they crossed the road. Which was quite unnecessary, she thought, as there was no traffic.

But she was glad they were crossing the road so they didn't have to walk past the newly-erected hoardings round the empty shops next to the theatre. All was quiet now, but on Monday morning the men would be bringing in sledge-hammers to start the demolition. A shudder ran through her and her hand tightened convulsively on Nicholas Dewer's arm.

Suddenly aware that she was clinging to him, Sally tried to snatch her hand away, but his hand closed over it, holding her firmly.

"Cold?" he asked.

The silk shawl she had borrowed from Anita wasn't much protection in the chill October night, but the touch of his hand was doing peculiar things to her pulse-rate, spreading warmth throughout her body.

"No," she said, hoping he would stop holding her so close to him. "I was thinking about the demolition."

"The shops?" He shrugged. "Surely they were no asset."

"Perhaps not," she conceded. "They're rather old-fashioned and due for refurbishment. It's the theatre I'm worried about." She lifted her chin. "We won't let them do it. They can't pull it down!"

"So you said earlier."

She frowned at his disinterested tone. She expected more enthusiasm. "But surely –" she began.

"Here we are," he said, releasing her hand. "The White Hart."

They had reached the eighteenth century granite build-ing at the corner of the square. Sally tried to adopt a nonchalant air as they entered the foyer. She glanced around surreptitiously at the oak panelled walls, deep leather armchairs and large evergreen plants in brass tubs placed strategically to give pockets of privacy, taking it all in so she would be able to describe it to her grandmother when she got home.

The blonde receptionist perked up immediately on sight of Nicholas Dewer's imposing figure.

He turned to Sally. "Would you like a drink?"

She shook her head. She hadn't eaten since lunch-time and it would be sheer lunacy to drink on an empty stomach. She was going to need all her wits about her.

"Not for me, thank you, Mr – er – Dewer."

"Nick," he said.

She could cope with that; it was his surname which made her uneasy.

"Let's eat then." He put his hand under her elbow to escort her into the restaurant.

Sally tensed. What was there about this man that he could throw her into confusion by his merest touch?

The restaurant was almost deserted and they were shown to a table in a softly-lit alcove. Sally smiled with delight. He was treating her like a real actress. A bouquet of red roses, now an intimate supper for two. She slipped off her shawl and draped it over the back of her chair before turning her radiant face to him.

"Hungry?" he asked.

"Starving," she admitted. "I always am after a performance."

He flicked a finger negligently at the menu. "Most of that won't be available – or edible – at this time of night. I suggest soup, followed by a steak and salad, if that's OK by you."

"Lovely." She was so hungry she was ready to accept anything.

She watched Nick beckon imperiously to the waiter hovering nearby and give their order. He really was the most impressive-looking man. His hair was pitch black, without a trace of grey, so he was probably in his early thirties, she decided. That tan hadn't come from a holiday in this country; the summer had been far too dull and wet for that. He must have spent some time abroad. Perhaps he was a playboy with a villa on the Mediterranean. His hands were tanned and capable, they gave nothing away.

She looked up and found his dark eyes on her. He was returning her scrutiny!

"Even lovelier without the greasepaint," he said softly. "But unusual colouring for Juliet."

Sally fingered a lock of her long blonde hair. "Authenticity isn't so important in Shakespeare. There were probably some fair people in Verona in those days. Besides," she added with a grin, "Sue, who's playing Lady Capulet, would have had a fit if she'd been asked to dye her hair black. Good wigs are expensive."

His gaze dipped to the low neckline of her gentian-blue dress. "You must have to spend quite a bit on costumes."

She straightened the cutlery on the table in front of her, unsure how much to tell him. But if he was going to help the theatre, he ought to know their financial state.

"We have the basic wardrobe available, which we can

adapt. But we usually make our own." She sighed. "We can't do Shakespeare very often. The cast is too large and it takes a lot of organisation."

The waiter came with their soup. When he had gone, Sally asked, "You're keen on Shakespeare?" Then cursed herself for such a stupid question. Of course he was. He had come twice to see *Romeo and Juliet*.

"It's an important part of our culture. I like to hear good lines well spoken." His eyes were telling her that he liked the way she had spoken them.

She glowed with pleasure. This was praise indeed. He must surely have seen all the best actresses on the London stage.

"Have you been acting long?" he asked.

"I've always been keen on the theatre. I joined the Dramatic Society as soon as I was old enough, while I was still at school."

His eyes twinkled with amusement. "Can't have been very long then. You're hoping to go professional?"

She shook her head. "The life's far too precarious."

He raised a cynical eyebrow. "Your parents wouldn't approve?"

A flicker of pain crossed her face. It was seven years since the tragedy but she couldn't bear to think of it even now. "I wouldn't like the travelling. I prefer to stay at home."

He studied her for a moment. "You must have a very interesting job."

She looked down at her plate. She couldn't possibly tell him she worked with her grandmother, growing herbs and keeping bees. He would think her a country bumpkin.

"I don't have a regular job."

"So you're really just a dilettante."

Sally laughed. "I wouldn't class myself as that!" But if he

thought she was, she must convince him of her sincerity.

Between mouthfuls of soup, she told him about the plays the Dramatic Society had performed, the parts she had played. And as she talked, her blue eyes sparkled with enthusiasm. Nick said little, but his eyes never left her face.

After the soup, the waiter brought the steaks, and a bottle of red wine which he showed to Nick for his approval, then poured a little into a glass.

Sally's eyes were drawn to Nick's mouth as he slowly raised the glass and took a sip. A sensitive mouth, she thought, then was suddenly filled with an inexplicable longing as the tip of his tongue moved slowly across his upper lip. She quickly looked away, lest he should read her errant thoughts.

She gazed around the restaurant while the wine was approved and poured out. There was only one other table still occupied, a group of men deep in discussion at the far end of the room.

"Most people dine much earlier," Nick said, drawing her attention back to him. He raised his glass. "To you, Sally Penrose."

She couldn't accept that toast. She raised her glass. "To The Duke's Theatre. Long may it prosper."

Nick turned his glass in his long fingers. "Is it prospering now?"

"That depends on what you mean by prospering, Nick." She took a sip of wine and put the glass down carefully. "There's a lot of activity. Plays, concerts, opera –"

"Does it make money?" he asked curtly.

"Er – well – not really."

"You mean, No."

She shrugged helplessly. "The building's old. It needs a lot of maintenance..."

"No doubt." He picked up his knife and fork. "Don't let

your steak get cold."

The steak was very succulent and she savoured every mouthful. "Mm, it's very good," she murmured.

He didn't reply. He was watching her in a way that made her very much aware of her own body, aware that she was a woman and he was a very attractive man. She couldn't hold his gaze and had to look down at her plate.

But he didn't let her escape his magnetism for long. "The Duke's Theatre," he mused. "Which duke?"

She had to lift her head to answer him. "It wasn't a real duke. He was a local landowner."

She forced herself to smile in an attempt to appear at ease. "It was an affectation of the aristocracy in the eighteenth century to open small theatres, so they could satisfy their own vanity in the guise of entertaining the peasants."

She swallowed. "Well, we didn't have the aristocracy, or the theatres." It was becoming increasingly more difficult to talk coherently with Nick's dark eyes upon her.

"The Cornish are independent folk. We have more than our share of eccentrics...."

He nodded encouragingly, and she went on. "Er – one of the local dignitaries fancied acting in his own theatre. He called it The Duke's." She added lamely, "With himself as the duke, of course."

"Of course," Nick repeated softly. He reached across the table and took her hand. "Are you one of those independent-minded Cornish, Sally?"

She touched her tongue nervously to her lips, and saw desire flare in his eyes. She knew now why he had wanted to talk to her in private. And she, naive fool, had thought he want to talk business!

"I – I was born in Cornwall," she stammered, unable to tear her eyes away from his. He wasn't asking her, he was telling her. His intention was clear in his eyes, those dark deep eyes that held her in thrall.

The moment stretched, stretched....

Then a shadow fell across the table. Nick withdrew his hand and the spell was broken.

A tall sandy-haired man said, "Nick, I didn't know you were here. Why didn't you come and join us?" But his grey eyes swept over Sally, giving his own answer.

Nick threw him a reproving look. "Hallo, Tom. Meet Sally Penrose. Sally, this is Tom Caldicot, my right-hand man."

"Trying to seduce the opposition?" Tom said softly, then turned to Sally. "Delighted to have the chance to meet you, Miss Penrose. I thought your Juliet quite enchanting."

"Thank you," she said automatically, glancing from one man to the other. Nick looked perfectly at ease now, so did the newcomer. But what was going on?

Tom leaned over her confidentially. "I ought to warn you. Nick eats little girls like you for breakfast."

She asked cautiously, "What do you mean, opposition?"

Tom laughed and slapped Nick on the shoulder. "Secretive devil." His eyes danced with amusement. "Hasn't he told you who he is?"

She glanced warily at Nick. He had asked questions and she had done most of the talking. "He's told me very little."

Tom grinned hugely. "Nick's our chairman and chief architect."

She frowned. All those qualifications. The A's hadn't been for accountant, as she had thought. But why was an architect interested in The Duke's Theatre? There was nothing special about the building; grey granite walls, crenellated at the top, and a slate roof, typical of the eighteenth century, but there were far better examples in the town.

Then Tom dropped his bombshell. "N. D. Construction. We're going to build the new supermarket."

Sally blenched. "You're what!"

Tom waved his hand towards the window overlooking the street. "We've just put up the hoardings, ready to start demolition...."

But Sally was no longer listening to him. She turned disbelieving eyes on Nick.

"You're the man who wants to pull down the theatre!"

He nodded. "It's almost falling down now –"

"And you let me think –! How could you!" She leapt to her feet. "So my first instincts were right. You are the Devil, Mr Dewer!"

He raised a cynical eyebrow. "Old Nick."

She waved her hand dismissively. "That makes you doubly evil. It's your other name. Dewer the Devil."

He glanced a question at Tom, then at her. "What do you mean?"

Her blue eyes blazed with fury. "You come here, eager to destroy our traditions, and you don't even know what they are!"

Both men were watching her now.

"Some Cornish fairy tale," Nick scoffed.

"Not Cornish. It's Devonshire. Dartmoor, to be precise." Sally glared at him. "Dewer is the Devil who rides with the Wisht hounds. Dewer is the Devil who lures travellers to their death on the Dewerstone!"

She pointed her finger accusingly. "And you, Mr Dewer, are the Devil who wants to destroy our heritage!"

She lifted her chin. "But you won't do it. This is war, Mr Dewer. We'll fight you to the end. And *we* will win!"

With a defiant toss of her golden head, she strode from the room.

Two

Her fury carried Sally out of the hotel and across the street. Of all the underhand, arrogant, conceited –! He had the gall to flatter her and lure her out to dine with him, getting her to talk about the theatre. And he wanted to pull it down!

Not if she had any say in the matter! She had been working hard for the campaign, she would redouble her efforts now. But there was so little time.

As she reached the corner, a cold wind whipped against her bare arms, making her shiver, and she realised with a pang that she had left her shawl – Anita's shawl – in the restaurant.

Sally glanced back at the floodlit facade of The White Hart. She couldn't go back. She had made a dramatic exit; she was too good an actress to ruin it by returning on such a trivial errand. She could phone the hotel when she got home. She wasn't going to speak to Nicholas Dewer again. Not tonight. Not ever!

But he might come after her if he noticed the shawl. She turned quickly and dodged down an alley. The town was a maze of narrow streets and winding alleys, and Sally knew it intimately. She made her way swiftly to the carpark at the rear of the theatre.

Nicholas Dewer might know where she had parked her car and come after her, but she was so cold she had to waste precious seconds rummaging in her tote-bag for her sweater. Hastily pulling it on, she glanced around. She could hear footfalls. Had he come after her?

She switched on the headlights, startling a courting couple in the lee of the theatre wall, and dazzling a shock-headed teenager taking a short-cut through the carpark.

Sally drove slowly to the main road and glanced up and down, but there was no tall dark man searching for her. She turned away from the centre of the town and drove the ten kilometres to the isolated cottage where she lived with her grandmother.

Monday morning saw Sally in town again.

After making her normal delivery of honey and fresh herbs to the health store, she drove to the carpark at the back of the theatre. Several members of the campaign committee had already arrived and they waved in greeting.

As she got out of her car, a Land Rover drew into the space beside it and Jake Treherne jumped down.

"Hi," Sally called. "I've got something for you, Jake."

He grinned. A hard-working curly-headed country boy of twenty-three, he couldn't resist playing the wicked squire when he was with friends. His gaze swept over her slim figure, clad in anorak and jeans. "Any time, m'dear. Any time."

"I thought we could do with some new placards." She glanced at the one Anita was holding, which read, 'Save The Duke's Theatre. Sign a protest now.'

"Something a bit more definite," Sally said, opening the hatchback of her Micra.

Everyone was watching as she pulled out a large placard and turned it to face them. It bore a caricature of Nicholas Dewer, with horns and a tail, thrusting a trident at the theatre building. Written in large black letters was, 'Don't let Dewer destroy our town!'

Jake frowned. "That's the man who came to the Green Room on Saturday."

Sally nodded grimly. "The boss of N. D. Construction."

Anita gasped. "The developer!"

Jake's blue eyes narrowed. "What did he want then? I mean...."

Sally flushed. Jake and Anita both knew that Nick had asked her to have supper with him. "Soft soap," she said bitterly. "He thought a bit of flattery and a good dinner would soften me up and I'd tell him our plan of campaign so he'd know what he's up against."

"You didn't!"

"Of course not!" Her chin came up. "What do you think I am!" She turned back to her car and pulled out another placard.

This one also had a caricature of Nicholas Dewer and it read, 'Save The Duke's from the Devil. Send an objection now.'

Jake nodded. "Dewer the Devil. I don't think he's going to like it."

"We don't like what he's doing." She handed Anita a cardboard box. "Grandma's typed another batch of objections, all slightly different of course."

Anita grinned. "Good. The planning committee will have to read every one." She chuckled. "It's a marvellous idea. So much more effective than a petition. I don't suppose they'd even bother to count the number of signatures."

"They have to list every one of these," Sally said. "We must make sure nobody signs more than one."

Jake moved away to begin organising everyone. As soon as he was out of earshot, Anita murmured, "Was it awful on Saturday night? I mean, the man looked genuine."

"He laid on the charm all right." Sally clenched her hands. "When I found out who he was, I lost my temper and stormed out. I'm afraid I left your shawl behind. I've phoned The White Hart but it isn't there. He must have taken it."

Anita shrugged. "Not to worry. I'm not desperate for it."

Sally turned thoughtfully to close her car. Nicholas Dewer was bound to return the shawl sometime. She hoped he chose a public place; she didn't want to be alone with him.

Jake came over. "You drew the placards, Sally. You'd better carry one."

"Try and stop me. I'll take the Devil one." She stood the placard upright. "The demolition crew should be arriving any minute. I thought we'd picket their entrance."

"Good idea." Jake glanced at Anita. "You'll take the other one?"

"I'm supposed to be on the objections. We must catch people on their way to work."

He waved his hand dismissively. "Sue can do that. You and Sally get our message across to the men who're doing the damage."

As the two girls set off, Anita glanced at the drawing on Sally's placard. "You're not usually vindictive, Sally. Did he make a pass at you?"

Sally was shaken. Was it vindictive? "He was the perfect gentleman, very flattering about the play." She clutched her placard as the wind caught it at the corner of the building. "He knows exactly what I think of him."

"You never lose your temper." Anita's eyes glinted. "Wish I'd been there to see it."

"Ham acting of the worst kind," Sally said disparagingly, hoping to close the subject. She didn't want to discuss it with anyone, least of all Anita, who was a bit of a gossip. "We're just in time. Look!"

A bright yellow truck was pulling in to the kerb.

"Come on," Sally urged.

The two girls quickened their pace and took up their positions on either side of the gate in the hoardings just as a burly red-headed man stepped down from the cab.

He paused, fishing in his pocket for the key, then gave a rapid double-take as he saw the placards.

"Hey, what's this then?"

Sally gazed at him in wide-eyed innocence. "We're exercising our democratic right to protest."

"Democratic right, eh?" He pointed to the Devil on the placard. "That's slander, or libel, or something, isn't it?"

"No," she said sweetly. "It's not defamation of character either."

"Humph." He glanced at Anita, a very pretty girl with curly black hair and big brown eyes she knew how to use, but she regarded him steadily. He turned again to Sally. In anorak and jeans, with no make-up and her fair hair drawn back in a ponytail, she looked so young he obviously considered her a harmless kid.

"Well, make sure you don't get in the way."

"No, sir," she replied respectfully, hoping she wasn't overdoing the innocent act.

He pursed his lips thoughtfully, then turned to unlock the gate.

A young man jumped down from the back of the truck. "A welcoming party?"

He was wearing jeans and a red check shirt with the sleeves rolled up to display his brawny tattooed arms. He looked Anita over very slowly, his gaze lingering on her shapely legs nicely revealed by the short black skirt she wore for her job as a waitress.

"Very nice," he murmured. "Very nice." And she fluttered her eyelids at him.

A man in overalls came round from the far side of the truck. He grinned when he saw the placards.

"Save The Duke's from the Devil," he read. "It's a good likeness."

"Cheeky," the tattooed man said, his eyes still roving over Anita.

"The boss won't like it."

The red-headed man called from inside the gate, "He'll like it even less if we don't start work on time. Get a move on, you layabouts."

"Our charming foreman," the cheeky one said with a wink at Anita.

They let down the side of the truck and began carrying their gear onto the site, stopping on each trip to chat with Anita, ignoring Sally as they thought she was only a kid.

With the arrival of the truck, a small crowd of sightseers began to gather. The men started playing to the audience, making a show of rippling their muscles as they lifted their tools from the truck.

"The Duke's?" the cheeky one asked. "Is that the pub?"

"No." Anita pointed. "It's the theatre next-door."

"The theatre Mr Dewer wants to pull down," Sally said in a clear voice that carried to everyone in the crowd.

The man glanced at her, then looked Anita over. "You an actress?"

"Sometimes," she said coyly.

"Oh-ho." He leaned closer. "Have you heard the one about what the bishop said to the actress?"

Her gaze swept over him in disbelief. "You can't fool me. You're not a bishop!"

He grinned, and there was a burst of laughter from all around.

Suddenly a commanding voice cut in. "What's going on here?"

The men were galvanised into action, hastily carrying the last of their equipment into the site, as the crowd parted and the tall figure of Nicholas Dewer appeared.

Sally swallowed, and lowered her head. He looked just as devastating in his working clothes of black jeans and denim jacket, with a yellow hard-hat tucked under his arm.

His black eyes scanned the scene, lingering on her and the placard she was clutching, before he turned to the sightseers.

"There's nothing to see, folks. I suggest you go about your business."

As he strode through the gate in the hoardings, people began to whisper.

"It's him, the Devil on the poster...."

"... he's the boss...."

"... going to pull down the theatre next...."

"No!" Sally protested. "We must stop him. Go and sign an objection. In the theatre foyer."

"Now?"

"Yes," she urged. "It won't take a minute."

A few folk exchanged glances, then walked towards the theatre; the others began to drift away.

"What do we do now?" Anita asked.

Before Sally could reply, Nick came striding out. He glanced around. "Everyone gone? Good. I want a word with you, Sally Penrose."

She jerked up her head and looked him in the eye. "I have nothing to say to you, Mr Dewer. I told you, this is war. We fight to the bitter end."

"You're causing an obstruction," he said evenly. "That's a civil offence."

"We are not! Anita and I are simply holding a peaceful protest. We can't help it if your employees wish to make an exhibition of themselves."

He jabbed his finger at the placard. "And you don't call that provocative!"

"A play on words." She kept her expression bland. "There's no point in making a protest if you don't catch people's attention."

"You drew that," he accused. "Nobody else in your set knows I'm N. D. Construction."

She raised one eyebrow. "Are you so ashamed you have to hide behind your initials?"

His jaw tightened. "I am not ashamed! It makes for easy identification. And there's the implied pun – deconstruction – showing that we do demolition as well."

"But not our theatre!"

"Huh!" he snorted. "That old heap of stones."

Sally drew herself up to her full height. "Now look here, Mr Dewer –"

"No. It's about time you took a good look –"

Anita had been eagerly following this exchange. "Time!" she exclaimed and glanced at her watch. "Wow! I must go, Sally. I daren't be late for work again." She passed the placard awkwardly from hand to hand. "What can I do with this?"

"Give it to me." Sally took the placard and stood it back to back with her own. "Thanks, Anita. Same time tomorrow?"

"Er – I dunno, I'll let you know." She gave Nicholas Dewer a tentative smile. "Sorry, I must fly."

"I'll tell Jake –" Sally began, but Anita was already walking briskly away, her high heels clicking on the pavement.

"Now we've dispensed with the distractions," Nick

said, "I'm going to talk some sense into that pretty little head of yours."

"Typical!" Sally snorted. "You mean you expect me to agree with you. Never, Mr Dewer –"

"It was Nick on Saturday," he said softly.

She didn't want to remember the way she had been deceived. "That was before I knew we were enemies."

"Of all the stubborn –" He sighed with exasperation. "At least come and look at the theatre from a surveyor's point of view."

"All right," she said. After all, there was no harm in looking. She lifted the two placards but the posts were rather bulky and she had to clutch them with both hands.

"You can't carry both of those. And I'm certainly not going to carry one. Leave them here."

"What! And get them trampled on. There's two perfectly good fencing stakes there."

He glanced at her wryly. "Not to mention your works of art."

"I believe in conservation. I don't like to waste anything."

"Especially not old buildings that are almost falling down." He took the placards from her, placed them firmly face to face and carried them through the gate to stand them against the hoardings on the inside.

The red-headed foreman was working on the front of the nearest old shop and must have heard most of what they had been saying. The look he gave Sally showed he was none too pleased that he had been conned into thinking her a harmless kid.

"They'll be safe there," Nick said. "Come on."

He strode off along the walkway and Sally would have had to run to keep up with him, but she deliberately lagged behind. She didn't want to be seen fraternising with the enemy.

He waited impatiently at the end of the hoardings and pointed up at the theatre building.

"See those cracks. The granite is crumbling away."

She knew that some old granite did eventually decay into china-clay, but this wasn't a clay area.

"It's a bit weathered," she admitted. "But what do you expect after two hundred years? It's a good strong building on a solid foundation –"

Nick laughed scornfully. "There aren't any foundations."

"Don't be ridiculous," she retorted. "Of course there are."

He shook his head slowly. "There aren't, you know. I've had a detailed surveyor's report. It's not unusual with buildings of this age." He waved his hand to indicate the other side of the street. "Most of those shops are newer, or they have cellars, which means foundations. But you'll find that many of the old stone cottages around don't have foundations. They were built straight onto the soil."

She didn't know enough about it to argue on that point. "Well, that doesn't mean it's falling down!"

He turned abruptly. "Can we go inside?"

"Yes, it's unlocked. We're using the foyer."

The glass doors were propped open to encourage people to come in. Sue, the platinum blonde who had played Lady Capulet in the play, was seated at a table covered in papers.

She smiled as Sally came in. "Your Devil placards are very effective." She patted a pile of envelopes. "We've had a good response." Her eyes lit up as Nick followed. "You've brought another –" She broke off as she recognised him from the placards. "Er – perhaps not."

"Definitely not," he assured her.

"Mr Dewer wants to convince me that the theatre is in imminent danger of collapse," Sally said sarcastically.

Sue glanced around in alarm. "It isn't, is it?"

"Of course not! It's been standing for two hundred years. It's not going to fall down now." Sally opened the door to the auditorium with elaborate courtesy, but Nick was looking at the papers on the table.

"So this is how you've done it. Snowed them under with paperwork." He ran his fingers through his thick black hair. "Decisions postponed three times. And I blamed Tom." He smiled grimly at Sally. "But you won't get away with it this time. I'm going to the meeting myself."

"And you, of course, can work miracles," she said sweetly.

"I'll have a darned good try." He glanced around in disgust. "But it'll take more than a miracle to save this place from decay. I'll show you what I mean."

He strode past her into the auditorium, and she felt for the light switches.

"There." He pointed. "Look at those damp patches on the wall. And there. And there."

Sally gazed at the dark stains on the faded murals. "Condensation," she stated defiantly. "The place isn't heated during the day."

"Faulty roof," he said. "And the plaster's crumbling away." He smoothed his hand over the architrave round a door. "And look here. Woodworm."

She glanced at the doorframe. "I can't see any."

"Of course you can't if you stand so far away." He caught her arm and pulled her closer, almost pressing her nose to the woodwork.

With his hands on her, she couldn't see anything clearly. "All right," she conceded, trying to pull out of his grasp.

He turned her to survey the auditorium. "The roof

beams are rotten." He sniffed. "You can smell the dry-rot. The whole place is in an advanced state of decay."

"Rubbish!" she protested. "You're making it all up. There's nothing wrong with this building that a bit of redecorating can't put right."

He glared at her. "Of all the pig-headed –"

He bit off the epithet he was tempted to use. "You're so blinded by sentiment you won't see any of the faults."

"And you're so prejudiced and steeped in building regulations," she retorted, "you can't see anything else!" Jamming her hands on her hips, she glared angrily at him, her blue eyes blazing.

Nick stood rigidly defiant, his jaw clenched, his black eyes boring angrily into her. Then suddenly his expression changed.

"Oh, yes I can." He grasped her shoulders and drew her towards him.

Sally was so startled she had no chance to resist before his head lowered and his lips met hers. She put her hands on his chest to push him away, but his jacket was unbuttoned and she could feel his heart beating under her hands. And all her anger melted away as she was swept by an excitement she had never felt before. Her head was reeling, her pulse was racing. The taste of his lips was intoxicating. She was drowning, drowning....

But this was madness. She couldn't let him do this to her. She hated him!

Suddenly gathering her wits, she jerked her head aside and pushed him away.

"Take your hands off me!"

He was breathing hard. "You're beautiful when you're angry," he murmured.

"Can't you think of something more original!" she snapped. "Typical male! Resorting to strong-arm tactics when you're losing the argument."

His eyes narrowed dangerously. "I was not losing the argument."

"Oh yes you were. Making up all those lies just because you want to build your horrible supermarket." She glared mutinously at him. "We've got plenty of shops. We don't need a supermarket."

"This town's dying on its feet. It needs more commerce." He jabbed his finger at his own chest. "If I don't build the supermarket, someone else will. So this building is doomed anyway."

"No!" she wailed. "It's our theatre. You can't pull it down."

He stared at her for a moment, then he seemed to come to a decision. "If you can't see with your own eyes what's wrong with it, come and look at the surveyor's report."

She glanced around at the damp patches on the walls. Was the building in as bad a state as he said? She knew they had been spending a lot of money on maintenance. Perhaps she should see the report if only to get some idea what repairs they ought to do. But she wasn't going to give in meekly.

"All right. So long as it's genuine."

Nick snorted, and strode out, holding the door open so she could see her way after switching off the lights.

Sue looked up eagerly as they came into the foyer but, at Sally's grim expression, she prudently didn't say anything.

Sally marched determinedly behind Nick out of the theatre and along the road. But he didn't stop at the gate in the hoardings.

"Were are we going?" she demanded.

He took her arm and escorted her across the road. "To The White Hart. I have the surveyor's report in my suite."

Sally stopped dead. "Not on your life! I'm not going up to your room!"

He sighed with exasperation. "Good grief, woman. It's mid-morning. I use my sitting-room as an office, with people coming and going all the time."

She suddenly felt rather foolish, but after his behaviour in the theatre, she didn't trust him.

"I don't know...."

"You'll have to come up anyway. You left your shawl on Saturday. It's in my room."

Anita's shawl. She didn't have any choice. "Oh, all right. But no strong-arm tactics."

His eyes twinkled with a smile he couldn't suppress. "You'll be perfectly safe. I promise."

"Huh! Nothing's safe from you," she muttered as she followed him into the hotel.

His suite was most luxurious, almost like a small apartment, with a large sitting-room furnished with plenty of armchairs, small occasional tables, and a desk which must have been put there specially for him, Sally decided, as it was of a different style to the rest of the furniture.

Nick strode across, picked up a big folder and handed it to her.

Sally gazed in bewilderment at the typewritten pages packed with facts and figures.

"Do you understand it?" he asked.

She looked up helplessly. "I don't even know where to begin."

He placed the file on the desk. "Here, I'll point out the salient parts."

She had to stand beside him while he explained it to her, but she found it more and more difficult to follow as his arm kept brushing against her, making her far too aware of him, as he turned the pages of the report and reached over to underline the relevant paragraphs with his finger. It was very dismal and she was sure he was picking out the worst bits.

When he reached the last page, she drew away and said brightly, "Well, you've given me something to think about. But I mustn't take up any more of your time."

Nick laughed shortly. "You and your friends have wasted weeks of my time. A few more minutes won't make any difference. Would you like coffee? I can have it sent up."

She wasn't going to risk being alone with him any longer. "No thanks. I'd like my shawl, please."

"It's in my room. I'll get it."

As he turned to the door, it opened and a striking auburn-haired woman came in.

"Oh, Nick. Have you seen my jade ear-rings?"

"You've probably left them in the bathroom again," he said gently. "You really must be more careful, Gill. We're not at home now."

She opened her hands apologetically. "I'm sorry darling. But you know how it is –"

He patted her arm affectionately. "I'll have a look."

Sally turned hastily to the desk as the colour drained from her face. She had seen the woman's wedding-ring. Nick was married! And he had his wife with him!

Three

"I'm sorry. Have I interrupted?" the woman asked.

Sally took a deep breath. She was going to need all her
stage training to turn calmly and face Nick's wife. Beauti-
fully groomed, in a chic black suit with a jade brooch on the
lapel, she was just the sort of sophisticated woman Nick
would choose.

Sally placed her hand on the file on the desk. "I was
looking at the surveyor's report, Mrs – er –"

"Masters. Gillian Masters."

So she wasn't his wife. But she was obviously sharing
his suite. At The White Hart too! He must be paying the
landlord handsomely.

Lovely amber eyes glanced at the desk. "I'm always
telling Nick he works too hard, but he's very keen to build
this supermarket –"

"Too keen," Sally said before she could stop herself.

"So you're one of the people who are holding him up."
Her gaze swept over Sally. "You're a bit young to be
leading a campaign."

"It's a joint effort." She hesitated. Should she admit her
age? She didn't want this woman to suspect that Nick had
kissed her – and not as he would kiss a child. "I'm nineteen, and thoroughly steeped in the Cornish tradition."

"But my dear," Gillian said kindly. "You're not making
the best of yourself. With the right clothes and skilful
make-up, you would look far more grown up."

Sally smiled. She had seen make-up transform Anita

into an old nurse, and she herself had played a goblin in pantomime.

"I haven't introduced myself. I'm Sally Penrose, a member of The Duke's Theatre Dramatic Society. We've been doing *Romeo and Juliet* for the past two weeks."

"I'm afraid I didn't see it." She studied Sally for a moment. "You were Juliet?"

"That's right."

Gillian nodded in understanding. "So you're deliberately playing the innocent schoolgirl this week. Very cunning. I can see you're going to give Nick a run for his money."

"We'll fight him every step of the way," Sally said, liking this woman in spite of herself.

Gillian laughed. "Nothing I enjoy more than a good fight. You know, Sally, I think you and I are going to be friends."

Nick appeared in the doorway and Sally was mortified to see that he had Anita's shawl over his arm. Gillian must surely guess how he had come by it.

"Found them," he said, holding out a pair of jade earrings. "On the dressing-table, behind a jar of face cream." He dropped them into Gillian's outstretched hand.

She smiled gratefully at him. "Nick, you're an angel."

A fallen angel, Sally thought, the Devil himself. Living with a woman – a married woman at that – yet he had definitely propositioned her on Saturday, and he had kissed her only half an hour ago. Had he no moral ethics at all!

Gillian turned to the mirror above the cocktail cabinet and put in the ear-rings. "I'm going shopping in Plymouth. I'll be taking the Porsche."

"Drive carefully, my dear." Nick kissed her cheek. "Have a good day."

"I intend to." Gillian went to the door. "Goodbye, Sally. I'll see you around sometime."

"Sure," Sally said awkwardly. She couldn't understand Gillian at all. Surely she wasn't so besotted with Nick that she couldn't see his real nature? Admittedly he had been gentle with her, but didn't she know that no woman was safe with him? Or did she think that Sally's schoolgirl appearance was insurance against him?

As the outer door of the suite closed, Nick said softly, "Thank you, Sally."

She glanced up at him in bewilderment. "For what?"

"For not allowing your antagonism for me to influence your treatment of Gillian."

"Well really! Just because I'm not a sophisticated city slicker like you, it doesn't mean I have no manners at all!"

He shrugged apologetically. "I'm sorry, I –"

"Anyway, there's no reason why I shouldn't like her," Sally said tautly. "She's not plotting to pull down The Duke's Theatre."

His dark eyes became speculative. "Is that all you have against me?"

The arrogance of the man! "No, it isn't!"

He was moving closer. She stepped back, but not quickly enough. He put his hand under her chin and lifted her face to look into her eyes.

"What else is there?"

"If you want the whole list, we'll be here all day!" She tried to pull away but his fingers tightened on her chin, holding her firmly.

"Tell me just one thing," he urged, his gaze lingering on her lips.

He was going to kiss her. She couldn't let him. It was only a moment since he had kissed Gillian. On the cheek, admittedly, but a real kiss would have smudged her perfect make-up. Sally wasn't wearing any make-up. That didn't mean he could kiss her instead!

"You said no strong-arm tactics," she protested.

His mouth was getting closer, his breath fanning her cheek. "Gentle persuasion," he murmured.

"No! Just because I'm a woman you think you can –"

The insistent high-pitched bleep of the telephone cut into her words.

"Damn," he muttered, releasing her to reach for the phone.

"Dewer here," he barked. "Oh, what is it, Tom?" His eyes suddenly hardened. "Trouble?" He stared at Sally. "Where?"

Her blood ran cold. Surely nobody had been so stupid as to interfere with the demolition work. From Nick's thunderous expression she knew he was going to blame her. Not likely! She had nothing to do with it. She wasn't going to stay here and get the full force of his fury. She grabbed Anita's shawl from the chair where he had dropped it and made for the door.

"Wait!" he called.

But she was off, running down the stairs.

Sally slowed her pace at the first landing and walked almost casually into the foyer, nodding politely to the receptionist as though she was one of the guests, then made her way outside.

She glanced up and down the road, but there was nothing out of the ordinary, so she cut briskly along to the demolition site. The gate was closed and pedestrians were walking past; a woman with a baby in a pushchair, an elderly man with a shopping-bag. Nothing to cause alarm.

Sally stopped outside the gate, listening carefully, but could hear only a light tapping sound, certainly no distur-bance. Perhaps it was in the square.

She hurried back past The White Hart and into the square. Here again, everything was peaceful as usual, people going about their normal business. Jake stood at the kerb handing out leaflets to the passengers alighting from a bus drawn up at the stop.

There was no trouble anywhere here; it must be in one of Nick's other enterprises. So why had he been glaring at her? Was it because he had been foiled by the phone?

Whatever the reason, she had escaped his clutches. And she had retrieved Anita's shawl. She had better give it back straight away.

The Copper Kettle was fairly busy when Sally went in. She hesitated at the door and glanced around. Anita was serving coffee and cream cakes to a group of middle-aged women, so Sally dropped onto a vacant chair and picked up the menu.

"I'll have coffee and a scone," she said when Anita came to her table. "I've got your shawl. Can you take it now?"

"Thanks." Anita raised one eyebrow. "Mr Dewer didn't have it tucked in his hard-hat this morning."

Sally wasn't going to tell her she had been to his suite. Heaven knew what Anita would make of that. "I had to go to his office."

"Wish I'd been there. Your row was just getting interesting when I had to dash off."

Anita wrote on her pad, then slipped the shawl over her arm and went out the door at the back.

She brought Sally's coffee. "He's very successful they say. Rolling in money." Anita wriggled her hips. "Think he'll look my way?"

Sally had to smile. It was a standing joke that Anita was after a rich husband.

"I should think you've got as much chance as anyone." She wasn't going to tell her he already had a woman with him. "But would you sell your soul to the Devil?"

Anita grinned. "I'd sell anything for a gorgeous hunk like him."

She wouldn't need to. One flutter of those expressive eyelids and he would get the message, Sally thought as she cut through her scone and spread each half with butter.

She was taking the first mouthful when Jake came to her table.

"What's this? Slacking?"

She smiled. "You too."

He dropped onto the chair facing her, reached over and took the other half scone from her plate.

"Hey," she laughed. "That's mine."

He bit into the scone. "You wouldn't deny a starving man."

"That'll be the day." She turned to catch Anita's eye and beckoned her over.

In her best waitress voice, Anita asked primly, "What can I do for you, sir?"

Jake leered. "What an interesting question."

She sniffed in disapproval. "You're lowering the tone of the establishment."

"In that case, I'll have to be satisfied with two scones and a cup of coffee, m'dear."

Sally watched in amusement. They played this scene, with variations, whenever Jake came to The Copper Kettle.

Serious again, he turned to her. "How did the picketing go?"

"It was quite successful. Sue said there was a good response."

"The Devil himself? What did he think?"

"He wasn't very pleased." Sally leaned forward. "Jake, he's had a survey done of the theatre."

She told him what she could remember of the survey, pausing to pinch half of one of his scones when she had finished her own.

"I think he was showing me all the worst bits to try to undermine our resolve."

"Never," Jake said. "But if it's as bad as you say, we'll have to launch a restoration fund."

"We've got plenty of support."

"We'll need it." Jake finished the last of the scones and drained his coffee cup. "Come, Sally m'girl. We've got work to do."

Slipping a generous tip under his plate, he picked up her bill and took it with his own to the till.

"You shouldn't have done that," Sally said as they left The Copper Kettle.

"You're an independent cuss, Sally Penrose, but I'll treat you if I want to."

"Thank you for the coffee," she murmured. "And the compliment."

Jake was unusually silent as they walked towards the square. Then he said softly, "I saw you going into The White Hart with Mr Dewer."

Sally jerked up her head. "I told you, he showed me the surveyor's report. He's using his sitting-room as a temporary office."

Jake scuffed his foot on the pavement. "He's rich, he's handsome. I – um – thought you were going over to the opposition."

Sally studied him for a moment. She liked Jake – everyone liked Jake – and she couldn't believe that he really doubted her devotion to the cause. There was more to his attitude than she was prepared to analyse right now.

She put her hand on his arm. "You know me better than that, Jake."

He leered, in his wicked squire manner. "Not as well as I'd like to, m'dear."

Glad he was not taking it any further, she smiled. "You've got a one-track mind."

"Not only one," he said lecherously, ogling a pretty girl crossing the road.

Sally burst out laughing. "You're hopeless."

They were both laughing so much, they didn't see the man coming round the corner and Sally walked straight into him. She gasped as the breath was knocked out of her and she almost fell to the ground. But strong arms shot out and caught hold of her. As she was hauled upright, Sally knew instinctively who it was. Nicholas Dewer!

She lifted her head. "I'm terribly sorry –" she began, but broke off as she saw his thunderous expression.

His dark eyes bored into her for a moment, then he put her firmly from him. He nodded curtly, "Miss Penrose. Mr Treherne," and strode away.

Jake watched him go. "Not very pleased, you said. He looked murderous!"

Sally was shaken. Did Nick think they were laughing at him? Or was he furious at the way she had escaped from his office?

"Public enemy number one," she muttered.

"He's a formidable opponent, Sally. He'll bring all the big guns to bear."

"But he's in alien territory, Jake. And we've got native cunning on our side."

"True." Jake nodded. "We'd better get on with it."

He turned towards the square and Sally set off in the direction of the theatre.

As she passed the demolition site, she noticed that the gate was open and stopped to look in. The red-headed foreman was working just inside.

"Excuse me," she called. "Mr Dewer put my placards inside for safety. May I come and get them, please?"

The man grinned. "Sure. He said you'd be wanting them." He pointed. "Against the wall there."

Sally stepped inside, picking her way carefully over some debris, and at first she couldn't see anything. Then her jaw tightened as she saw the two stakes – with nothing on top of them!

She turned to the grinning foreman. "Very funny. Where are my placards?"

He pursed his lips. "Mr Dewer said you were very particular to have those. Two perfectly good fencing stakes."

He was quoting her own words back at her. "Yes, but what about –"

His expression went blank. "Mr Dewer put them there."

Mr Dewer no doubt took the placards off them as well! A formidable opponent indeed.

She wasn't going to get anything out of the foreman so she smiled sweetly at him. "It's very kind of you to take care of them for me."

And shouldering the stakes, she marched out to her car.

Sally was exhausted physically and mentally when she drove home that evening. As she approached the white-washed stone cottage she recalled what Nick had said and wondered if it had been built straight onto the soil with no foundations. She must ask her grandmother.

Parking her car in the garage, she took out the two stakes and leaned them against the wall, then closed the door against the cold night air before going into the house.

Her grandmother, a tiny woman with bright blue eyes and pure white hair, turned from the cooker as Sally came into the spotless all-electric kitchen.

"Hallo, love. Been a long day. How did it go?"

Sally's eyes softened as she was swept by the deep love she felt for her grandmother. She knew that, if it wasn't for her, she too would have perished in the fire seven years ago which had claimed her parents. This little woman had risked her life to save the grandchild she loved, and she still bore the scars.

Sarah Penrose never went into town, but she was keenly interested in what was going on.

"We got a lot more objections," Sally said.

"Good." Her grandmother smiled. "Dinner's practically ready. You can tell me all about it while we eat."

"I'll nip upstairs and have a wash."

When Sally came down again, her grandmother was carrying a tureen of home-made soup to the highly-polished table in the dining-alcove where they had their meals. Although they lived in complete isolation, Sarah Penrose had been careful to maintain standards of etiquette so that Sally grew up knowing how to behave.

When they had tasted their soup, Sally began eagerly relating the happenings of the day, making the story come alive so her grandmother could share her experiences. Usually she didn't hold anything back, but she couldn't tell her grandmother how Nick had kissed her in the theatre; she didn't quite understand herself how it had happened.

"...And when I went to collect my placards, do you know what he'd done! Taken them off, so all I got was the stakes!"

Mrs Penrose smiled. "Well, you didn't expect him to like them. You can easily make some more."

"Horrible man." Sally scowled. "I wish I'd told Anita he had a woman with him. It'd be all over town by now and he'd be hounded out."

"You wouldn't like that, dear. If you start playing dirty, it'll come back at you tenfold." She nodded wisely. "If we play it straight, I'm sure we can win."

Sally was thinking what Anita had said. "Grandma, do you think my placards were vindictive?"

Her grandmother considered. "Rather naughty, but not vindictive. You must remember, Sally, it's the principle you're fighting. Mr Dewer's plans, not the man himself."

Sally glanced at the red roses in the vase on top of the bookcase, the bouquet he had given her on Saturday. She thought of this morning in the theatre, his dark eyes glaring at her, then softening with desire, and unconsciously touched her tongue to her lips as she recalled the way he had kissed her.

She didn't see her grandmother frown as she said softly, "It's Nick I have to fight, every moment of every day."

Four

The following day was market day, and the last day of the campaign. The ancient charter forbade political activity in the pannier market, so there could be no placards or picketing inside.

Sally finished arranging the jars of honey she had brought for the health-food stall, then she placed a card in front of them. At first glance it looked innocent enough; a water-colour sketch of The Duke's Theatre. But in Gothic script, she had written, 'Don't let commerce destroy our heritage. Object now. Tomorrow will be too late.'

She smiled as she stepped back to admire her handi-work. If anyone in authority noticed, it would probably be thrown out, but plenty of people might have read it, and acted, before then.

"It's pretty," a feminine voice said, and Sally spun round to meet lovely amber eyes.

"Mrs – Masters," she stammered. "I didn't know you were there."

"Gillian, please." She pointed an elegant finger. "Did you draw that?"

Sally nodded.

Gillian leaned closer to read the legend, then she smiled. "Neat."

Her gaze swept over Sally, who was once more dressed in anorak and jeans, a complete contrast to Gillian's stylish navy suit.

"You're very talented, Sally. An actress and an artist.

Yet Nick said you're unemployed."

Sally was amazed. Why on earth had they been discussing her? She glanced around hastily. Was Nick here?

"He's had to go to Exeter," Gillian said. "Trouble on one of the sites." She waved her hand towards the health-food stall. "You work here?"

"No, I'm just keeping an eye on it while the stall-holder's busy." She wasn't going to explain her way of life. "I'm not unemployed. I don't work regular hours."

"Freelance?"

"You could say that." Why were they interested? Surely Nick wasn't going to offer her a job!

Gillian studied her for a moment, but didn't press the point. "I love markets like this. All sorts of stalls mixed up together."

"There's a kind of logic in it," Sally explained. "Mainly food – fruit, vegetables and such – up this end, with most of the handicrafts at that end. It saves getting the serious shoppers hampered by the browsers."

"I'm really a browser," Gillian said. "I'm looking for a nice present for Nick."

Sally reached behind her and picked up a jar of honey. "Give him this. He's going to need sweetening after the planning meeting next week."

Gillian raised one eyebrow. "A peace offering?"

"Not likely! It's war to the finish."

She put the honey into her bag. "I'll give it to him with your compliments."

"Tell him it's a sweetener for the bitter pill of defeat."

Gillian laughed, and Sally watched her walk away, then mentally kicked herself as she realised what she had done. Her address was on the label. She had as good as told Nick where she lived!

"Any customers?" The stall-holder had returned from

parking her van.

"Only one jar of honey." Sally fished in her pocket for the money. It was easier to pay than explain that she had given it away.

She helped putting out the rest of the merchandise, then she was free to concentrate on the main business of the day. She was heading out of the market building when she met Jake coming in.

"I'm not slacking," Sally said before Jake could get a word in. "I've got to put my car in for service, then I'm on duty in the square."

"Placards again?"

She nodded. "I've made a new one. Don't worry. It's not controversial."

Jake grinned. "The others were very successful."

Sally was about to move on, when he added, "I've got tickets for Saturday. Will you come to see *Carmen*?"

She smiled. "I'd love to. We must support our own theatre."

He asked casually, "Shall I pick you up?"

Sally shook her head. "There's no need. It's too far out of your way. I'll meet you at The Duke's."

They both knew it wasn't strictly true, but Jake accepted it, as did all her friends, who assumed it was because of the bees that she never invited anyone to her home. They couldn't know that she had seen people's revulsion when they first caught sight of the right side of her grandmother's face, and she loved her too much to subject her to that humiliation again.

Sally thought back to the time, seven years ago, when they had first moved to this area. The scars had been livid then and, knowing she was marked for life, Sarah Penrose had wanted somewhere to hide. She had found the cottage, which was isolated yet not too far from a village. There was a two-acre plot of land as a buffer round the cottage, and she had studied books on beekeeping and bought several hives as further protection from the curious. Later she began herb-growing, always wearing her beekeeper's hat with its heavy veil whenever she went outside.

Although Sally had been only twelve then, she had done all the shopping, and she had been delighted at the friendliness of the local people. They always asked after her grandmother, and Sally was often given new-laid eggs, pots of home-made jam, or a freshly-baked sponge cake as gifts for her. It was a complete contrast to the way she had been treated before, and Sally was glad they had moved here.

Mrs Penrose never went out, so Sally did all the errands, including changing books at the mobile library, which came to the village once a fortnight.

Her grandmother was very interested in history and folklore, and one day, when they had been living there about a year, Sally had collected some books on Dartmoor legends. She had just gone down the library steps when she heard two elderly women talking inside.

"Dartmoor, eh? Gonna find some new spells."

"They turns theysen to a black dog and goes owling over t'moor all night."

"Er wears that 'at to 'ide er orrible face."

"And so un can't see when er gives un the evil eye."

Sally had been absolutely shattered. She knew enough about folklore to understand what they meant. They were talking about her grandma! Saying she was a witch!

It hadn't been kindness that had made them ask after her. It was superstitious fear. All those gifts had been to keep her sweet, so she wouldn't put spells on them!

After that, Sally wouldn't accept anything from anyone. She became very independent, and fiercely protective of her grandmother, never allowing anyone to come to the house. She persuaded her to put some beehives along the front drive to frighten callers away, and had an intercom installed so that she never had to answer the door.

For many years, no one else had set eyes on Sarah Penrose, except perhaps from a distance as she worked in the garden or handled the bees, and she was always protected by the heavy veil of her beekeeper's hat.

The scars had faded now, but they were a constant reminder to Sally of the love her grandmother felt for her, a love which might have cost her her life.

Walking back to her car, Sally remembered the library books she had promised to return. She smiled as she lifted out the heavy bag. For the past few months, she had borrowed everything she could find on planning regulations, ancient monuments, historic buildings, and her grandmother had pored over them, trying to find any loophole in the law, any- and every-thing they could do to prevent a decision on The Duke's Theatre and save it from demolition.

It had been her grandmother's idea to provide ready-typed objections, all slightly different. It had worked so far. They had managed to delay decisions three times. She only hoped their efforts succeeded again and they had another reprieve.

After dropping the books in at the library, Sally checked in her car at the garage, remembering to take her placard out first. In bold black capitals, it read, 'Don't let them demolish The Duke's. Object today. Tomorrow will be too late.'

She sighed. If she had known that Nicholas Dewer was going to be out of town, she would have drawn another Devil. But at least there was no danger of him trying to put a stop to her today.

It was cold and blustery, so Sally was glad of her anorak and warm sweater as she paraded slowly up and down the square, then later outside the hoardings round the demolition site. The sky gradually clouded over as the day wore on, and a light drizzle was falling by four o'clock when the campaign officially ended.

Jake fell into step beside her. "Knocking off time. Your placard's beginning to smudge."

"Yours too," she said. "Good thing the weather's held till now."

"Perhaps the Fates are on our side," he suggested.

Sally frowned. "It'll take more than that to beat the Devil."

They walked together back to the theatre, where the other campaigners were checking in.

Jake leaned his placard against the wall. "Well, this is it, folks. The end of this phase of the campaign." He looked around, making eye-contact with each person in turn. "Everybody's worked hard, we've done all we can." He shrugged. "There's not much point in hanging about now. See you all at the council meeting next week."

"Sure." There was the usual chatter as folk began to drift away.

Sally went to the table where Sue was hastily gathering up all the objections they had obtained that day. "I'll take those, if you like. I've got to collect my car and the office is on my way."

"Would you," Sue said gratefully. "I'm in a bit of a rush. I've got to pick up the girls from school."

"You go. I'll tidy up here."

Soon everyone else had gone and only Jake and Sally were left.

She tucked the envelopes into her bag. "It's a bit of an anticlimax when it's all over, isn't it?"

Jake nodded. "Dad'll be pleased. I'll be pulling my weight on the farm again." He opened the door for her and they walked together out into the drizzle.

"It's been fun," he said. "Let's hope we've been effective."

"Oh, we mustn't lose," Sally said fervently.

Jake looked down into her eager blue eyes, then his own eyes brightened.

"Sally," he murmured and, putting his hands lightly on her shoulders, he lowered his head and kissed her.

Sally was surprised, but not startled. Jake had never kissed her before, except on stage. And this was about as exciting, she thought as he drew away.

"See you Saturday," he murmured, and turned towards the carpark.

"Bye, Jake," Sally called and turned in the opposite direction.

As she walked briskly along, she couldn't help remembering that other kiss, yesterday, in the theatre. The feel of Nick's lips upon hers, the taste of him, the scent of his skin. It had been pure magic – and she didn't even like him!

But she did like Jake. She had known him for years. Perhaps that was it. He was a friend, they were accustomed to one another; there couldn't be any excitement with him.

She cut across town to the council offices and handed in the objections well within the deadline. Her duty was completed. All she had to do now was to collect her car and go home.

But when she reached the garage, Sally was dismayed to find her car still up on the ramps.

The mechanic came out from underneath, wiping his hands on a paper towel. "I'm sorry, Miss Penrose. I've been rushed off me feet all day. Only just started on it."

She frowned. He had said, "four hours", when she had checked it in. "How long –?"

He related a catalogue of disasters, men called out on emergencies, and one man having to be rushed to hospital after an accident in the workshop.

"I can get it done tonight, if you're pushed."

She didn't want to hang about that long. "It's all right. I can go home by bus."

He said earnestly, "I'll bring it out in the morning as soon as it's ready."

She couldn't have that. "If you're short-handed, you won't have the time. I've got to come in to town tomorrow anyway," she lied. "Give me a ring when it's finished and I'll collect it."

"Thanks, Miss Penrose," he said gratefully. "I'm terribly sorry about this...."

Sally turned away and trudged back up the hill. The drizzle was developing into steady rain. Not the best sort of evening to get stranded without her car, she thought as she pulled up the hood of her anorak. Especially as she would have a kilometre to walk at the other end of the bus journey.

But even that prospect faded into insignificance as she reached the square just in time to see her bus pull away from the stop. There was a good hour's wait till the next one.

Sally stood on the corner and cursed herself for a fool. She should have insisted that the garage lend her a car to get home. But the mechanic had been so distraught she hadn't even thought of it. Should she go back? Or hire a cab? Or go and get a cup of coffee while she waited for the bus?

She was trying to decide when a sleek black car drew in to the kerb. The passenger door was pushed open and a familiar voice said, "Hop in."

Sally stood rooted to the pavement. Nicholas Dewer! "You can't be here," she said stupidly. "You're in Exeter."

"Obviously not. Well, come on. It's pouring with rain. You'll get soaked."

She didn't want to get into the car. He had been furious when she had last seen him. Where was he going to take her? "But – I –"

"I'm going your way. I'll give you a lift."

"No!" She drew back hastily.

"Oh, for goodness sake! Get in. I'm on a yellow line. Do you want to get me arrested for kerb-crawling!"

Sally glanced around and saw that people were beginning to stare. She made a sudden decision. She would ask him to overtake the bus and drop her off at a convenient stop.

"Oh, all right." She scrambled in and slammed the door.

"Fasten your seat-belt," he ordered tersely as the car slid away from the kerb.

She obeyed, then pushed back the hood of her anorak. It was an ordinary navy-blue anorak. She studied Nick's hard profile.

"How did you know it was me? A lot of people have anoraks like this, and I had the hood up so you couldn't see my face."

He threw her a cynical glance. "My dear Miss Penrose, you have certain attributes which are quite distinctive. I daresay I could recognise you in a nun's habit."

Which didn't say much for her acting ability, she thought. "I might have been waiting to cross the road –"

"But you weren't."

How did he know? "My car –"

"Is in dock," he said firmly.

Sally began to feel uncomfortable. Her blue eyes narrowed angrily. "Have you been spying on me?"

"Not intentionally."

When he didn't elaborate, she asked sharply, "What do you mean?"

Nick put up a warning finger and she realised that the indicator was flashing. He needed all his attention on the traffic to negotiate a right turn. He was wearing a grey business-suit, she noticed, so whatever he had been doing in Exeter it wasn't on a building site.

When they were safely round the corner, he said, "I wasn't spying on you. I pulled in for petrol at the garage down the hill and happened to overhear the tail-end of your conversation with the mechanic." He threw her a wry glance. "I wouldn't expect you to give in so easily."

"Give in? There was nothing to give in to. The poor man's had a disastrous day."

Nick snorted. "And you believed his sob-story."

Sally said icily, "He's an honest hard-working man. Not that you'd be able to recognise one! In a small town like this, people trust one another."

"Mugs," Nick said. "Anyway, he let you go off on foot in the rain."

Sally watched the windscreen-wipers sweeping back and forth. Maybe Nick had a point there, but she wasn't going to blame the mechanic.

Nick said, "That's how I knew it was you on the corner. And you missed the bus."

"It's just ahead." Sally pointed. "If you overtake it, you can drop me at the next stop."

"Oh yeah," he said sarcastically. "Now you're going to tell me you live right by a bus-stop."

"Well, not quite." Even though it was pouring with rain, she would rather walk a kilometre than have him take her right home.

"How far?"

"A short distance," she said vaguely.

He raised one eyebrow. "A hundred metres? Two hundred?"

"Er – a bit more than that."

"Good grief woman! Do you have to be so stubborn! Are you ashamed of your home?"

"Of course not! It's a very nice cottage." She glared at him as the car swerved out to overtake the bus. "I didn't ask you to give me a lift. Stop here and I'll catch the bus."

"So you can catch cold walking home in the rain. What sort of monster do you think I am!"

As Sally opened her mouth to reply, he added quickly, "No, don't answer that."

"Why not?" she couldn't resist asking. "Afraid of a few home truths?"

He ignored her taunt. "I know your address, but I'm not quite sure where it is. You'd better direct me."

"How did you find it?" she asked, already knowing the answer. He must have been back to the hotel and seen Gillian.

He smiled grimly. "I always make a point of reading the small print. Even on a jar of honey."

She didn't have to admit it, she would get him to drop her somewhere nearby. "It doesn't have to be my address."

"But it is."

It wasn't a question, it was a statement. He must have been checking up on her, so there was no point in trying to deny it.

"Yes," she said softly. "Turn left at the next junction."

As he slowed for the corner, he said, "On Saturday you gave me the impression that you're unemployed. Why didn't you tell me you're a honey farmer?"

She wasn't going to admit that she hadn't wanted to appear unsophisticated. "Why didn't you tell me you're a property developer?" she countered.

He laughed suddenly. "Touché."

Her breath caught in her throat. He was so wickedly handsome, with an aura of maleness which was overpowering in the close confines of the car.

She leaned forward to stare out through the rain-washed windscreen, concentrating on pointing out the route so she didn't have to look at his face. But she was still very much aware of his lithe body seated beside her, his thigh almost touching her own.

"A bit lonely out here," he commented as they drove down a narrow winding lane between moss-covered stone walls, overhung by the delicate drooping branches of beech trees. There were very few gates and no houses.

"It's lovely and peaceful," Sally said defensively. "I believe one can be very lonely in a block of flats in the centre of a city."

Nick shrugged. "I suppose it depends what you're used to. Have you always lived in the country?"

"I couldn't live anywhere else," she said evasively. She wasn't going to tell him about her childhood. "There's a T-junction ahead. Turn right."

There were no lights showing in the cottage, she noticed as he drew up at the gate. Her grandmother must be in the kitchen at the back.

Sally unclipped her seat-belt. "Thank you for the lift," she said, reaching for the door handle.

Nick was staring at the cottage, the small-paned windows dark against the whitewashed walls, the random pattern of the granite blocks glistening wetly in the rain.

He snorted. "I can see now why you're so fanatical about old buildings."

"Well, there's nothing wrong with this one," she retorted. "You're not going to demolish it."

"Georgian," he mused. "Stone and rubble wall construction. No foundations. I'll bet it's damp."

"It is not!" She glared at him. "You're too keen to pull things down. Don't you know anything about renovation? The previous owners had it completely damp-proofed."

His lip curled cynically. "And no doubt destroyed all its olde-worlde charm."

She wasn't going to mention the oak beams in the ceilings and the lovely old staircase, or he might want to see them. And she definitely had no intention of letting him get any closer to the house than he was now, parked outside in the lane.

"It's extremely comfortable and very easy to run."

"But not very inviting." He pointed to the beehives lining the drive. "Those must put off any visitors."

"That's the idea. They're far more effective than a guard dog."

Nick turned to her, his dark eyes searching her face. "Sally?" he asked incredulously. "You don't live all alone out here?"

Her jaw tightened. "It's none of your business who I live with!"

He grasped her shoulders. "What if I want to make it my business?"

"No!" she breathed, panic sweeping over her. She knew it had been a mistake to let him bring her home. He was so inquisitive, so persistent. But she couldn't let him interfere with their lives.

"Please," she begged. "Please leave me alone."

His hands moved to cup her face and she was sure he could feel the frantic beat of her pulse.

"That's not what you really want," he said softly.

She stared wide-eyed at him. "Please, Nick," she begged. "I don't –"

"I thought you'd called a truce." He began gently stroking her cheek with his finger. "I haven't thanked you for the honey."

"That wasn't a peace offering," she said, hoping to divert him from asking about her home-life. "The war still goes on. The honey was meant to sweeten the bitter taste of defeat."

"Oh, but I'm not going to lose. Not the fight. Nor the opportunity." He slid his arm round her and drew her to him.

"No!" She put her hands on his chest to push him away.

But he was far stronger than she was. He crushed her to him and his mouth closed over hers.

At the touch of his lips, the thudding of her heart changed from fear to another, more pleasurable, excitement and her lips parted under his. She clutched at his lapels, but the kiss was so persuasive, instead of pushing him away, she found herself pulling him closer.

Her head dropped back as he kissed her cheek, her throat, then his lips were upon hers again. It was magical, making her feel so alive, so feminine. She had never been kissed like this before.

"Sally," he murmured. "You're so lovely, so sweet."

His tongue plundered the sweetness of her mouth, drugging her senses, and she was hardly aware that his fingers were feeling for the zip on her anorak. He smoothed his hand over her sweater, lightly brushing across her breasts, and her body responded instinctively.

Sally gazed at him in wonder. "Nick?" she breathed.

Taking this as encouragement, he slid his hand under her sweater.

She gasped as he touched her bare skin. "Oooh, your hand's cold."

"Sorry," he murmured, stroking over her sweater again to cup her breast. "Let me come in, Sally. Let me make love to you."

Let me come in. The words screamed in her brain. She jerked upright and pushed him away.

"No! No, you can't!"

"But Sally...." He reached for her again.

She backed away, glancing wildly around. "No. You shouldn't have come this far. You're a cunning devil, Nicholas Dewer, trying to charm your way through my defences."

She tugged up the zip on her anorak. "But you won't win."

His dark eyes narrowed. "Oh yes I will. This is only the beginning, Sally Penrose. What I want, I get."

"No." She flung open the car door and leapt out, slamming it behind her. Then she ran for the house.

When she reached the garage door, she stopped and turned back, but he wasn't following her. Not in person, only with his eyes. Those dark devil's eyes were fixed on her. She shuddered. He was far too sure of himself.

Then, to her relief, he started the car and drove away.

She stood in the lee of the garage long after the car was out of sight and she could no longer hear the engine. She breathed deeply to slow her racing heart and only when she was sure she could face her grandmother calmly did Sally turn to go into the house.

As she reached the kitchen door, she suddenly remembered that she hadn't told Nick how to get back to the main road. She had deliberately brought him by an indirect route, he might drive around these lanes for ages and never find his way.

A grin spread over her face. Serve him jolly well right!

Five

Jake gave a low whistle when he came into the theatre foyer that Saturday evening and saw Sally waiting for him. His admiring gaze moved slowly down her white sheath dress with a lace over-blouse, to her white high-heeled court shoes, then slowly up again to her fair hair piled elegantly on top of her head.

"Wow!" he breathed. "You've dressed like this for me."

Sally smiled. She wasn't sure what had prompted her to wear a new dress this evening. "And for The Duke's Theatre," she said lightly.

Jake couldn't stop gazing at her. "Perhaps I should have gone to Moss Bros...."

He was wearing his best dark-grey suit with a white shirt and a jaunty blue bow-tie, which suited his youthful good looks. Sally slipped her hand through his arm. "You look very dashing."

"And you look good enough to eat." He glanced towards the kiosk. "Would you like some chocolates?"

Sally laughed. "And risk ruining my dress? It's a lovely thought, Jake, but no thanks."

"I hadn't thought of that." He took the tickets from his pocket. "Shall we go in?"

They made a very attractive couple as they walked towards the auditorium, unaware of the tall dark man in a dinner-jacket who paused at the theatre entrance to watch them.

Greeting several friends and acquaintances in passing,

they made their way to their seats in the middle of the sixth row.

"This is nice," Sally said, as Jake put down the seat for her. "Near enough to hear well, but not so close you can see their make-up."

"Though when you've worn it yourself, it's not so off-putting," Jake said.

Sally opened the programme. "Oh dear. They've photo-copied photographs."

Jake leaned over, his curly head almost touching hers as they studied the programme together. "Good thing they didn't do that with us. Your sketches came out much better."

He sat back, and suddenly drew in his breath. "He's got a nerve! Coming here again now we know who he is."

Sally didn't have to ask who he meant. She raised her head to meet piercing dark eyes. Nicholas Dewer was about to take his seat in the front row.

"He's probably come to count the damp patches on the walls," she said bitterly. "Or maybe he's hoping the stage will collapse."

But Jake's attention had moved to the auburn-haired woman Nick was settling in the seat beside him.

"Who's that gorgeous-looking dame?" he murmured almost to himself.

Sally threw him a wry glance. "Her name's Gillian Masters."

Jake turned sharply. "How do you know? Have you met her?"

"I told you, on Monday. Ni – er Mr Dewer's using his sitting-room at The White Hart as an office. I went to see the surveyor's report. She was there."

"You mean, she's his secretary?" He turned again to look, but they had sat down and he couldn't see them. He gave a slow grin. "If he's got a secretary who looks like that, he can't get much work done. There's hope for us yet, Sally m'girl. We might win."

"We've got to win," she said fervently, all too aware that she was going to have difficulty concentrating on the stage now she knew that Nick was sitting only a few rows in front of her.

The Operatic Society had been working on *Carmen* for months, and all their hard work paid off. The simple sets were more than compensated for by the flamboyant costumes and very creditable acting. Everyone knew what to do and did it well. The town didn't have an orchestra but the rather unusual combination of piano and an assortment of strings, woodwind, a trumpet and drums gave ample support to the singers, and delighted the audience.

"Almost professional," Jake commented as the lights went up for the interval.

"Maggie makes a lovely Carmen," Sally said.

Jake grinned. "Maggie would make a lovely anything." He stood up. "Come, Sally m'dear. We'd best get to the bar before it runs dry."

She knew there was no danger of that, but it would be crowded.

"In that dress, you'll be wanting something a bit up-market," Jake mused as they entered the bar. "Sherry? Gin? Whisky?"

"No thanks. They put me to sleep. I'll have the usual, please."

"Right you are, m'dear. You stay here and I'll fight my way through the crush."

Sally had to smile. The idea of him having to fight his way was so ludicrous. Apart from a bit of friendly rivalry, there was never any pushing or shoving at The Duke's. She listened to the buzz of enthusiastic comments about the performance. The opera was being a success, *Romeo and Juliet* had been a success. Surely nobody could doubt the value of The Duke's. The town really needed this theatre.

There was a sudden silence. She turned – as did everyone else – to see a vision come in. Gillian was absolutely stunning in a purple Grecian gown with a heavy gold Cleopatra necklace, and her lovely auburn hair drawn up into a Grecian knot.

But it wasn't so much her arrival which had caused a stir. The patrons parted to make way for Nicholas Dewer as he went to the bar.

Gillian hesitated a moment, then smiled as she saw Sally, and came over to her.

"No innocent schoolgirl tonight," she murmured with a wink.

Sally wondered if she was aware of the atmosphere. "How are you enjoying the opera?"

"It's wonderful." Gillian glanced around but people had begun chatting again; there was no hostility shown to her. "I haven't been to amateur theatricals for years, and I must admit I didn't expect such talent. It's as good as some professionals I've seen."

Sally smiled shyly. "What a lovely thing to say."

"It's true," Gillian assured her.

Jake gaped and nearly dropped the glasses when he saw who Sally was talking to.

"Er – your drink, Sally," he stammered, his eyes on Gillian.

"Thanks." Sally took the glass from him before he could spill it all over her dress. "Jake, I don't think you've met Mrs Masters. Gillian, meet Jake Treherne. He was my Romeo last week."

"Any time, m'dear," he said with a strong Cornish accent, but it was purely out of habit. He was overawed by

Gillian's sophisticated glamour.

"I'm sorry I wasn't here to see it, Jake," she said kindly. "If it was anything like *Carmen* tonight, it must have been very good."

"Oh, I think we were adequate." He glanced at her empty hands. "Can I get you a drink, Mrs Masters?"

"Gillian," she corrected him. "No thanks. Nick's seeing to it." She looked at the large glass Sally was holding. "What's that you're drinking?"

"Cider." At Gillian's puzzled frown, Sally added, "Everyone in the Westcountry drinks cider."

Jake said, "It should really be scrumpy. That's rough home-made cider."

"And pretty rough it can be," Sally said with a grimace. And they all laughed.

"What's the joke?" Nick's deep voice cut in.

Sally caught her breath. She had known he would join them, but his presence was still a shock. He was far too overpowering – and too close. She stepped back a pace and Jake moved to stand beside her, defining the battle lines.

"Your drink, Gillian." Nick handed her a cocktail, then he raised his glass of whisky. "Your very good health," he said, his gaze moving slowly over Sally, making her tingle as though he had caressed her, and suddenly she knew why she had chosen to wear this dress.

"To The Duke's Theatre," she said defiantly, letting him know that the war went on.

Jake added, "Long may it prosper," as he raised his glass in salute.

Nick snorted. "Make the most of it while it lasts."

Sally met his cynical gaze. "We intend to."

Gillian glanced from one to the other, a slight smile on her lips. "What's your next production?"

"*Carmen* runs for another week," Sally said. "Then there are recitals. We're doing an Edwardian melodrama at the end of November."

"And we're all getting together for a pantomime at Christmas," Jake put in.

Nick asked dryly, "Where are you planning to perform these entertainments?"

Sally smiled sweetly. "Right here, Mr Dewer. At The Duke's Theatre."

Gillian pursed her lips prettily. "I haven't seen a pantomime in years. I'll look forward to it."

Jake couldn't keep his eyes off her. "You'll be here in December?"

"This is going to be my centre of operations," Nick said, his gaze fixed on Sally. "I'm looking for a suitable property."

"Georgian and damp," she said bitterly. "So you can demolish it."

"I'm thinking of moving here. I want somewhere to live."

"But you can't!" she gasped. The prospect was appalling. She couldn't risk running into him every day. She swallowed. "I mean – the town won't stand much of your kind of development."

"I've found an office in town, but I'm looking for a house in one of the outlying villages." He took a sip from his glass. "I'd like to learn more about the area. Would you two have supper with us after the show?"

Sally went as stiff as a ramrod. She couldn't possibly dine with him. Not after last time.

Jake slid his arm round her waist. "It's very kind of you, Mr Dewer, but it wouldn't be right. We're definitely on opposite sides, and we're not going to risk jeopardizing our position before the meeting next Thursday."

Nick's eyes narrowed slightly. "So be it. I was hoping you could tell me something about the local amenities."

"You're planning to destroy the most important of them," Sally retorted and, catching a gleam in Gillian's eyes, realised she was enjoying this enormously.

Nick studied the whisky in his glass. "There must be plenty of interesting places around, but it's easy to lose one's way in the narrow winding lanes."

So he had got lost on Tuesday! Sally suppressed a smile of satisfaction and said with feigned innocence, "It often happens to incomers. They get pisky-led."

Gillian smiled. "Pisky-led? I've never heard of that. What is it?"

"It's well known in Cornwall. If you upset the piskies, they lead you a merry dance and you never find your way. You can be lost for hours, days even."

"How fascinating." Gillian glanced at Nick, then at Sally, as though she knew there was more to this than casual conversation. "How do you get back again?"

"You have to break the spell," Sally said, conscious of Nick's glass swirling slowly in his long fingers. She began to wish she had never started on this. "You either turn your pockets inside out, or take off your coat and put it on inside out."

"Symbolising that they've turned your life inside out," Gillian said shrewdly. "But who are these piskies? Where do you find them?"

"You don't." Sally touched her tongue to her lips. "They're the little people who inhabit the moors and byways of Cornwall."

Nick drew himself up to his considerable height and looked down upon her. "Piskies," he said grimly. "So that's what you call them." He was telling her that he knew she had taken him by a round-about route then let him get lost on Tuesday.

She was saved from further embarrassment by the bell ringing for the end of the interval.

As they went back to their seats, Jake asked, "What was all that about?"

"Teaching them a bit of folklore," Sally said evasively.

Jake wasn't so easily put off. "There's something going on here that I don't know about. Has that man been bothering you, Sally?"

"No," she said quite truthfully. Bothering wasn't the word at all! "I think he's trying to intimidate us into giving in."

"He won't intimidate me," Jake said stoutly.

Having seen Jake handle the bull on his father's farm, she knew no one could frighten him, but his emotions weren't involved in this. She lowered her head to study the programme so she wouldn't see Nick going to take his seat in the front row.

The second half was just as good as the first, and the audience clamoured for encores. But none were given and eventually the enthusiastic applause subsided.

"Terrific," Jake said. "I must admit I don't usually go for opera, but *Carmen* doesn't really count, does it."

"It's got lots of jolly good tunes." Sally smiled wryly. "Not to mention the gorgeous girls."

"Not as gorgeous as you look tonight, Sally." His gaze swept over her white dress. "Let's do something special. How about supper?"

Sally tensed. Jake might want to show that he could stand up to Nicholas Dewer. "Not The White Hart."

Jake put his hand under her elbow. "I was thinking of driving out to The Halfway House."

"That'd be lovely," she said.

And it was. Jake had borrowed his father's Volvo to take

Sally to the charming seventeenth century inn. While they enjoyed a light supper of local trout served at a small table in the dimly-lit lounge, they chatted about anything and everything, but mainly the campaign and their hopes for the meeting on Thursday.

Then Jake drove Sally back into town to collect her car.

"I wish you'd let me take you home," he murmured, and putting his hands on her waist, he bent his head and kissed her.

Sally slid her arms round his neck, trying to respond, but as his lips moved on hers, she felt nothing. No excitement, no magic. It was just a kiss.

"Thank you for a lovely evening," she said as he raised his head. "I did enjoy it."

He looked down into her eyes in the dim light of the carpark. "Sally? I – er –"

She didn't want to encourage him. "We're friends, Jake," she said gently. "And we've got a lot of work to do. Let's not complicate matters at this stage."

"Right you are, m'dear." She knew he was disappointed, but he wouldn't show it. He stepped back. "See you Thursday."

"I'll be there."

All the campaigners were there, supported by several people who had sent in objections. They knew, under the council rules, they would not be allowed to speak, but they all wanted to see how the meeting went.

Sally was looking very businesslike in a tan suit and white blouse with a bow at the neck, and her hair drawn back neatly into a chignon. She sat between Jake and Anita, the attention of all of them focussed on the tall dark man in a charcoal-grey suit seated on the opposite side of the chamber.

Nick looked very confident. Too confident, Sally thought and wondered if he had some trick up his sleeve to outmanoeuvre them. What could he have done that they knew nothing about?

"Any idea who that chap is with him?" Jake whispered. "Do you think it's his lawyer?"

Sally glanced at the sandy-haired man in a grey suit who was talking in a low voice to Nick.

"Tom Caldicot," she whispered. "I don't think he's a lawyer. Nick called him his right-hand man."

Jake's eyebrows shot up. "Nick?"

She swallowed. "Er – a slip of the tongue." She invented quickly. "I think of him as Old Nick, the Devil."

"If he wins today, I'll wish him to the Devil," Jake muttered. "Oh good, they're going to start."

"I bet they keep us till last," Anita whispered as the officials began opening files and rustling papers.

Sally cast her eye quickly over them. Not one had looked at Nick, though they must know he was there, so she was sure that something was up.

Then the chairman broke with normal procedure and, instead of dealing first with unfinished business, began working slowly and laboriously through many new applications. Listening to the committee droning on, Sally was sure that Nick had been trying to push them. But these were true Cornishmen, they weren't going to be harried by a Londoner. They were being deliberately long-winded to make him wait.

But for what?

As the afternoon wore on, people began to get fidgety. Sally's eyes were drawn constantly to Nick. His confidence didn't seem to wane, but his impatience grew. Several times she saw him consult his watch, then make some comment to Tom Caldicot.

At long last the chairman said, "Finally –"

And everyone sat up eagerly.

"This is it," Anita whispered.

He cleared his throat. "Finally we come to the application held over from last month to allow for more consultation. The application by N.D. Construction for the demolition of the building known as The Duke's Theatre in order to make way for the building of a supermarket."

He tapped a very bulky file. "We have received many objections...." Then he went on and on, listing the main reasons for objection.

Nick was leaning forward impatiently, trying to urge him to get to the point.

"We have also received notification that petition has been made to the Department of the Environment...."

The campaigners exchanged puzzled glances. What was this about? Sally was surprised to see that Nick was frowning too.

"... with regard to classifying The Duke's Theatre as a listed building...."

A sibilant hiss traversed the chamber as everyone repeated, "Listed building."

Sally glanced at Jake, then at Anita as the implications began to seep in. She saw Nick's jaw tighten.

The chairman went on: "... until we receive clearance from the Department of the Environment, we cannot make any decision on this application."

"A reprieve!" A cheer went up from the campaigners.

Nick leapt to his feet. "May I ask who lodged this petition?"

All eyes were on the chairman as he consulted his notes. He mumbled the first name but the second was quite clear. "The signatory was Sarah Penrose."

Sally's eyes lit up. "Grandma!" she breathed.

But everyone thought it was her.

They began cheering and clamouring with congratula-
tions. "Sally, you're a genius!"

"Fantastic!"

"Brilliant!"

Everyone was shouting and talking at once, and the
noise was deafening.

"Order! Order!" the chairman called.

But nobody took any notice and the meeting broke up in
uproar.

There was a sudden hush as Nicholas Dewer strode
furiously across the chamber. People stood aside to make
way for him, and watched eagerly to see what would
happen.

He came up to Sally, his dark eyes boring into her.
"Piskies!" he growled. "I should have known you were up
to something!"

Sally was so elated she wasn't going to be cowed by him.
"I told you it was war, Mr Dewer."

"Listed building, my foot! The only list that building
should be on is of decaying death-traps!"

'It's all perfectly legal," she said, smiling up at him,
which only made him more furious.

He jabbed his finger. "It's just a delaying tactic. You and
your friends are costing me a fortune, Miss Penrose. Don't
you know, time's money!"

"Not here, it isn't," she answered defiantly. "You can't
buy two hundred years of history."

"Bunk!" he snarled and turned on his heel. "Come on,
Tom. We've wasted enough time here already."

Jake grinned. "That's told him straight. He can't do
anything for at least a month."

"We've won!" Anita glanced from one to another of the
group. "We ought to have a drink to celebrate."

Sally laughed. "We'll do better than that. Let's go right into the lion's den. Cream teas at The White Hart. Come on, everybody. It's on me."

As they walked triumphantly through the town, Jake fell into step beside her.

"Sally." He sounded rather hurt. "We've been working on this together for months. You could have told me."

She smiled and shook her head. "I didn't know."

He stopped and stared at her as though she was mad. "Don't be ridiculous!"

"It wasn't me, Jake. It was Grandma."

"He said Sarah Penrose. That's your real name."

"It's also my grandma's name," she explained gently. "That's why I'm called Sally."

"You mean –?"

She put her hand on his arm. "I'd never keep anything like this from you, Jake. You know that."

He searched her face. "You really didn't know?"

"Grandma's been studying all the books I could lay hands on and she's written dozens of letters. I thought she was only after information. I had no idea...."

Sally led the way into the restaurant at The White Hart. There was no sign of Nick. Probably gone up to his room to cool his temper.

She counted up. "Cream teas for ten," she told the waiter.

They were all in high spirits as they talked about future plans.

"The melodrama's definitely on," Jake said.

"And the Christmas panto," Anita added. "Government departments take ages to get round to anything."

Sally gazed round at their happy faces. How different it might have been if Grandma hadn't intervened.

As soon as they had finished their cream teas, she went

out to her car, eager to get home and tell Grandma how it had gone.

Once outside the town, she encountered very little traffic as she drove along the narrow winding lanes. But as she turned right at the final T-junction, Sally slammed on the brakes.

There was a black Porsche parked outside the gate!

Six

Sally sat motionless, staring at the Porsche. Nicholas Dewer! Was he in the car, or had he gone to the house? How dare he! Her blood began to boil. He had no right to come barging into her home!

She put the Micra into gear and drove slowly forward. As she reached the point where she had to turn, the door of the Porsche opened and Nick stepped out.

Sally had to make a rapid decision. If she drove in, he would follow. It was better to confront him out in the lane. She put on the brake and leapt out of the car.

"What are you doing here!"

"Waiting for you, Sally Penrose."

He was wearing a black sweater and looked very menacing in the half-light. She had to find out if he had been to the house.

"How did you know I wasn't already home?"

He came nearer. "Because you and your cronies were happily ensconced at The White Hart, celebrating your hollow victory when I left."

Thank goodness for that. She would never forgive him if he upset Grandma.

"I might have been staying out all evening."

"That was a risk I was prepared to take."

"What!" she scoffed. "And waste even more of your precious time."

"You're very good at wasting my time." He snorted. "A merry dance you led me when I brought you home last week."

Sally glanced around. "How did you find it today?"

He smiled maliciously. "Turned my car inside out, of course, and let the piskies drive me here."

He was getting closer, too close. She tried to step back but there was no room to manoeuvre in the narrow lane and she was up against her car.

"Well, what have you come for?" she demanded.

He glanced towards the house with its dark windows. "Isn't there somewhere more comfortable where we can talk?"

"You chose the venue," she said defiantly.

He turned to the Porsche. "Come and sit in my car, then."

"Not likely!" She wasn't going to risk getting that close to him again. "Say what you've come to say and get on with it."

"All right." He stood squarely in front of her, feet apart, put one hand in his trouser pocket and pointed at her with the other. "That petition of yours is a deliberate ploy to waste time. It hasn't a hope in hell of succeeding."

"Don't be too sure," she said with far more confidence than she felt.

"I've been checking the records. That building's only been a theatre for the past ten years."

"That's not true!" She glared at him. "It was very popular last century, and the early part of this."

"On high days and holidays." He stepped forward, his jabbing finger almost touching her. "It was used as an ordnance store during the war, then a furniture warehouse. It's only recently that anyone's taken an interest in it."

"It was built as a theatre, it's still a theatre," she declared.

His eyes narrowed ominously. "You will withdraw

your petition."

She threw back her head. "Never!" How could she when she hadn't the faintest idea what her grandmother had written, or to whom?

Nick stepped closer, but she had backed against the door of her car. He put his hands to either side of her shoulders, trapping her there.

"You will withdrew your petition," he repeated firmly.

Sally was suddenly afraid. They were alone in the middle of nowhere and she was utterly at his mercy. She took a deep breath and looked him bravely in the eye.

"Oh-ho. Physical intimidation again."

"I'm not touching you," he bit out. "Though I'm sorely tempted to put you across my knee and give you a good spanking. I've never come across anyone so stubborn, pig-headed –"

"Verbal abuse now!" she flung at him.

"You prefer physical?" He grasped her arms and jerked her towards him, then his mouth was on hers in a punishing kiss.

Sally was startled by his sudden move and went to throw up her hands instinctively, but she was crushed to his hard body and couldn't move.

As her head was forced back by the pressure of his mouth, she became furiously angry. He had no right to treat her like this! She clamped her teeth tightly together and went rigid in his embrace. She wasn't going to be crushed into submission.

His mouth ground against hers, but she was so angry she wouldn't yield. Then he changed tactics and his tongue moved sensuously over her lips, but she kept her teeth firmly clamped, determined not to give in, even though the scent and taste of him were weaving their usual magic and her body began clamouring to respond.

Sensing her inward struggle, he gave a low chuckle deep in his throat and moved his hands tantalisingly to stroke her neck, her shoulders and down her back. But she made herself ignore his caresses and remained stiffly resistant.

When he eventually lifted his mouth from hers, she said furiously, "Stop trying to bulldoze me, Mr Dewer! It won't work."

"Won't it?" he said softly, stroking her cheek.

"Just because I'm smaller than you, and female, you think you can treat me as you please. Well, I warn you, Mr Dewer, you'll regret it!"

He dropped his hands from her and stepped back. "What do you mean?"

She wasn't quite sure what she did mean, but at least she could breathe more freely now.

"I told you, the Cornish are very independent. We don't take kindly to incomers trying to tell us what to do."

He nodded knowingly. "Just as I said. Stubborn and pig-headed."

"Not as pig-headed as you are!" she retorted. "You've got one aim in mind. To build your rotten supermarket. If that means demolishing our theatre, you couldn't care less. You think our objections are just time-wasting, costing you money."

Her blue eyes flashed with fire. "You don't listen to us. All you do is try to crush the opposition. Well, you can't ride rough-shod over our committee. Or over me!"

She pointed imperiously at his car. "Now I think you'd better go!"

He stood his ground. "But I haven't finished with you yet."

"I have nothing more to say to you!"

She strode past him to the gate, but he caught her hand

and pulled her round to face him.

"It's no good losing your temper. Can't we talk this over rationally?"

"Rationally! Huh! You just want me to give in and agree with you."

Nick was now facing the house, and she tensed as his expression suddenly changed. What had he seen? Sally glanced over her shoulder. There was a light in a ground-floor window. Grandma must have gone into the lounge. But she always drew the curtains before switching on the light, so he couldn't have seen her.

"So you do live with someone," Nick observed. "But it can't be Treherne. He was with you at The White Hart when I left."

Her eyes widened in shock. He thought she was living with a man! Of all the –! She opened her mouth to protest, then snapped it shut again as the idea came to her. If she let him think that, he would have to leave her alone.

"Young fool," Nick scoffed. "Doesn't he know you're two-timing him?"

Sally drew in her breath indignantly. "What do you mean?"

"It's obvious." He looked down at her neat tan suit. "You're an actress, always playing a part, and you've been rather overdoing the innocent act lately."

He put his hand lightly to her cheek, making her quiver. She jerked her head away and his hand slid down, deliberately brushing her breast.

"You can't deny your passionate nature." He lifted his hand in a seemingly casual manner to brush her breast again. "No woman as innocent as you pretend to be would respond so readily to a touch."

And it was true; her body did respond immediately to him. To hide her confusion, she said furiously, "No man should expect to have exclusive right to every woman he meets."

"So," he mused. "You admit there's competition."

"I admit nothing." He was too persistent, too probing. She should never have got into this sort of argument with him.

"My private life is my own. Haven't you got enough women running after you without pestering me!"

"Pestering?" He pursed his lips. "That's not the word I would have chosen."

"I don't care what you call it. Just leave me alone. You've got Gillian –"

His eyes narrowed. "Don't you dare say anything against Gillian. She's had enough to contend with."

Sally snorted. "I'm not surprised, if she's living with you. Does she know –"

Nick caught her arms. "You leave Gillian out of this! I warn you, if you do anything to harm her –"

Sally was shaken by his vehemence. "Let go of me, you bully!"

His jaw tightened for a moment, then he suddenly dropped his hands and stepped back. Sally rubbed her arms where he had gripped them.

Nick was immediately contrite. "I'm sorry. Have I hurt you?"

"You wouldn't care if you had," she retorted. "You've got a bulldozer mind. You have to crush everything that stands in your way."

"That's not true," he said evenly. "I'd never deliberately hurt you, Sally. And I certainly don't want to crush you."

He glanced around. It was nearly dark now, the trees etched black against the sky, the only light being the faint glimmer through the lounge curtains, throwing into grotesque relief the beehives lining the drive.

"I came out here," he said, "because I wanted to talk to you alone."

"So there wouldn't be any witnesses while you brow-beat me," she snapped.

He leaned casually against the gatepost. "You intrigue me, Sally Penrose. You're so spiky."

She stepped back warily. "I don't like being waylaid outside my own home."

"That's what I mean. Why does it have to be outside?"

"Because I don't invite every Tom, Dick and Harry inside!" She clenched her hands. She daren't let him know she never invited anyone in. He was far too inquisitive; he would want to know why.

"But you know me." He put his hand on her shoulder, nearly making her jump out of her skin.

Sally glanced wildly from side to side. How was she going to get rid of him without raising his suspicions?

"I don't know you," she said anxiously. "Not that well."

He leaned forward and peered into her face. "What are you afraid of, Sally?"

She tried to pull away but his hand tightened on her shoulder. "I – I'm not afraid. I just don't like being man-handled."

He glanced towards the house. "I wonder...."

Sally was frantic. She had no idea how she was going to get out of this.

"You have no right –"

"I have every right –"

"No!" she cried. "Go away! Leave me alone!"

She thrust her arm up sharply, knocking his hand off her shoulder, then she turned and ran blindly into the darkness. "Leave me alone...."

Her heart was pounding in her ears as she raced up the drive and round the house to the back. She stopped, gasping for breath, when she reached the door. She daren't burst in upon her grandmother like this.

Sally leaned against the wall, taking deep breaths to calm her racing pulse. Then, as she reached for the door handle, she caught a glimpse of a dark figure coming round the corner of the house. Nick! He had followed her!

She shoved the door open and quickly stepped inside, but he had his foot on the threshold before she could slam it shut.

"Go away," she hissed, pushing hard against the door.

Nick put one hand on the door and forced it open. "You ran away. I wanted to make sure you're all right."

Bracing her hands against the doorframe to bar his way, Sally glanced anxiously over her shoulder into the dark lobby. He hadn't kept his voice down. Had her grandmother heard?

"I'm perfectly all right," she whispered urgently. "Leave me alone. Please go away."

There was a sound behind her. Sally spun round as the light went on, shining full upon her grandmother standing in the kitchen doorway.

For a moment everything froze, like a tableau. Then her grandmother gasped and put her hands to her face. But too late. Sally was sure Nick had seen the scars, the marks of love on her grandmother's face.

She rushed over and put her arms protectively round the little woman. "I'm sorry, Grandma. I couldn't stop him."

She turned fiercely to Nick. Dressed entirely in black, he stood tall and menacing, completely dwarfing the two women. But she saw no revulsion in his dark eyes.

He stepped into the lobby. "Aren't you going to introduce me, Sally?"

"That's hardly necessary," she said bitterly. "You

couldn't be anyone but Nicholas Dewer."

Mrs Penrose stared at him, her hands pressed to her cheeks. "Devil by name, Devil by nature."

Sally kept her arm round her. "This is my grandmother, Sarah Penrose."

Nick had begun to move forward, his hand outstretched, but he stopped in his tracks. "Sarah Penrose," he repeated thoughtfully, his gaze moving from one to the other. "That's what the chairman of the planning committee said. I thought he meant you, Sally."

"So did a lot of other people." She tightened her hand reassuringly on her grandmother's shoulder. "We won, Grandma. They've put it off for another month."

"Good. I'm glad it worked." She lifted her head. "I was the one who made the petition, Mr Dewer, so you can stop bullying my granddaughter."

Sally moved to stand protectively in front of her. "And you'd better not hurt my Grandma!"

Nick stood in the middle of the lobby, fixed by two pairs of bright blue eyes, one apprehensive, the other defiant, the family likeness very marked.

"I have no intention of doing so." He nodded formally to her grandmother. "I must apologise for this intrusion, Mrs Penrose. Sally and I were having a heated argument and I'm afraid I pursued the point a little too far. I hope you can forgive me."

He moved forward, offering his hand to Mrs Penrose, but Sally stood resolutely between them.

"It's all right, Grandma," she said. "You go into the kitchen. Mr Dewer is just leaving. I'll see him out."

She stood firm, hands on hips, glaring at him until she heard the kitchen door close behind her.

"I think you'd better go," she said coldly. "You've caused enough trouble for one day."

Nick ran his hand through his black hair, his eyes on the closed door. "Why the hell didn't you tell me you live with your grandmother! I thought –"

"I know very well what you thought. We don't all have the morals of an alley cat!"

His jaw tightened. "There's no need to be offensive."

"You can talk!" she exclaimed. "Barging in here and frightening the life out of my grandmother!"

He sighed. "I'm very sorry about that. Please give her my apologies, Sally. It's not my habit to go around terrifying old ladies."

"No, you prefer terrorising young women!" Sally went to the back door and held it open.

Nick stood looking down at her. "You know that's not true. Anyway, you're not afraid of me." He glanced around. "But you are afraid of something and I'm determined to find out what it is."

Sally stared at him. He had seen her grandmother's face. He must realise how Sally had been trying to protect her from humiliation. But he had to come bursting in!

"Go away!" she cried. "Leave me alone."

"No." He put his hands on her shoulders. "I want you, Sally Penrose. There's no way I can leave you alone. But now is not the time. You must go and reassure your grandmother."

He bent his head and kissed Sally firmly on the mouth, then strode away into the darkness.

She stared dumbly after him, feeling as though she had been run over by a bulldozer. When his footsteps had died away, she slowly closed the door, knowing that the cottage would never again be the safe refuge it had been all these years. It would take more than a door to keep Nicholas Dewer out!

Seven

Sally went into the kitchen to find her grandmother making a pot of tea and, for the first time since the scars had healed, she saw that the old hands were not quite steady.

Her heart was wrenched with anguish. "I'm sorry, Grandma. I did my best to keep him out."

"I'm sure you did, dear." Mrs Penrose carried the teapot shakily to the table. "Now, don't upset yourself. What's done is done." She was trying to comfort herself as much as Sally, and her blue eyes were anxious as she added, "It was bound to happen sometime."

Sally gritted her teeth. She would never forgive Nick for this. "It just had to be him!"

Her grandmother poured out the tea and handed Sally a cup. She took several sips from her own cup to steady her nerves before she replied, "Now I've seen the Devil himself, I have a better idea what we're up against. He's a very forceful character."

"That's a polite way of putting it!" Sally retorted. "He was absolutely livid at the meeting this afternoon."

Hoping to take her grandmother's mind off her recent trauma, she described in great detail what had occurred, emphasising to comic effect the long-windedness of the council, and even managed to make her grandmother smile at their tactics.

"That's why Nick waylaid me out here," Sally went on. "He thought I'd made the petition, and demanded that

91

I withdraw it. He says it hasn't a hope in hell of succeeding. Has it, Grandma?"

"I shouldn't think so, dear. But it's bought us some time."

"That's true," Sally agreed. "We must make the most of it."

They hadn't won yet, they only had a reprieve. The campaign must go on to make sure people didn't forget about The Duke's Theatre and let Nicholas Dewer win by default. She knew he wouldn't waste any time. Somehow she had to find out what he was going to do.

But her first duty was here at home; she must look after her grandma.

Sally kept an eye on her and noticed that she was rather subdued all evening and went to bed early, but next morning she seemed to have recovered from her ordeal and suggested they work in the garden.

There was plenty to do, hoeing, weeding and tidying the plants for the winter.

Sally was carting a barrowload of weeds to the compost heap when she stopped, her ears pricked. She could hear a vehicle in the lane. The engine note changed. It was drawing up outside.

Not Nicholas Dewer! He wouldn't dare come again!

She dashed round the side of the house, her heart thumping in anger. But as she reached the gate she saw that it wasn't the Porsche but a dark-green van with the name of a florist on the side. She let out her breath in a sigh. Somebody had got lost again. Putting on a placatory smile, she waited while a young woman came round from the far side of the van.

But to Sally's surprise, she smiled and held out a cellophane-wrapped bouquet.

"I hope I've come to the right place. Sarah Penrose?"

"Er – yes," Sally stammered. Who on earth was sending flowers? She signed the receipt automatically and hardly noticed the van drive away.

She gazed at the bouquet of huge yellow chrysanthemums. Then she saw the envelope pinned to the wrapper. On it was written in bold handwriting, 'Mrs Sarah Penrose'. And Sally knew who had sent it. Nicholas Dewer!

If it had been addressed to her, she would have thrown it straight onto the compost heap. But it was for her grandmother. She gritted her teeth and marched indoors.

Mrs Penrose always escaped to the kitchen if anyone came to the house, and Sally found her there, making coffee.

"For you, Grandma," she said, tossing the bouquet onto the kitchen table.

Her grandmother stared at the flowers in bewilderment. "For me?" Then she saw Sally's grim expression. "I suppose you know who sent them."

"I can guess."

"They're beautiful." She unpinned the envelope and slit it open. "We'd better see what he has to say."

Sally watched impatiently while her grandmother scanned the note. "Well?" she prompted.

Mrs Penrose cleared her throat. "Please accept these flowers as a token of my sincere apology for my unwarranted intrusion into your home last night...."

"Soft soap," Sally snorted. "He's just trying to get round you."

"...I would like to have the chance to discuss with you my plans for the redevelopment in the town centre...."

"Discuss! Huh! He doesn't know the meaning of the word. His idea of a discussion is to browbeat you into

submission." She glanced at the paper in her grandmother's hand. "Does he say when he wants this so-
called discussion?"

Mrs Penrose swallowed nervously and went on, "Would
you care to have lunch with me at The White Hart –"

Sally blenched. "How dare he! Adding insult to injury!"
She grabbed the bouquet. "I'd like to stuff his rotten
flowers down his throat."

Mrs Penrose put her hand firmly on Sally's arm.
"That's no way to treat flowers. They're only passive
messengers." She took the bouquet and placed it on the
draining-board. "I don't think losing your temper is
going to do any good. A bit of diplomacy is called for."

"Diplomacy! When he's deliberately trying to humiliate
you."

Mrs Penrose looked down at the white scars on the
backs of her hands. "Perhaps he doesn't know I never go
out...."

"But he saw you, Grandma."

"Yes, but –" She turned and went to a cupboard at the
far end of the kitchen to look for a vase. "The light was
poor. He might not have noticed...."

Sally gazed at the back of her grandmother's bent
head. Nick had thought she was living with a man. He
was so surprised to see her grandma, it was possible
that he hadn't noticed what she looked like, especially
as she had quickly covered her face.

"What are you going to do, Grandma?"

Mrs Penrose brought out a large glass vase, filled it
with water and arranged the chrysanthemums before
she spoke.

"I'll phone The White Hart –"

"You won't speak to him!"

"No, dear. I'll leave a message. I accept his apology but

decline his invitation."

He wouldn't let it go at that, Sally thought. He had waylaid her to try to get her to withdraw the petition. Now he knew it was her grandma, he would find some way to get at her.

She gazed at the chrysanthemums. Flowers were the first step, but now Grandma had refused his invitation, what would he do next? Would he come to the house? She would have to be extra vigilant and try to head him off.

For the rest of the day, while they worked in the garden, Sally was alert to every sound, rushing to the gate the moment she heard a vehicle in the lane. But none stopped. And the phone didn't ring.

She was sure this was only a breathing space. Nick was bound to do something.

Next morning she was raking up the autumn leaves scattered over the front lawn, her artist's eye delighting in their various colours and patterns, when she became aware of the purr of a well-tuned engine. Sally dropped the rake and dashed to the gate just as the black Porsche drew up outside.

Nick! And he was here!

She stood on the inside of the gate, her arms folded defiantly on the top, and watched him get out of his car. Tall and powerful, he was wearing a sweater and jeans, both of which were black. The Devil incarnate, she thought as his black eyes rested on her.

He smiled. "Good morning, Sally. It's a beautiful day."

"It was," she said bluntly.

His gaze flickered over her belligerent stance. "Tut, tut. And you told me you had good manners."

"When necessary, Mr Dewer." He was coming closer. Sally flicked a glance at the bolt. It was good and strong, he wouldn't be able to push the gate open. "Don't tell me you just happened to be passing."

"No. I'd like to see your grandmother. Is she in?"

Sally said coldly. "My grandmother is always in, but she does not receive visitors."

Nick looked up at the house. "You don't expect me to believe that."

"Believe what you like," Sally retorted. "But you're not going to see her."

"Don't you think you might ask her first?"

He put his hand casually on top of the gate and Sally suddenly realised that he was so tall he could easily vault it. She moved to bar his way.

"There's no need to ask. Grandma won't see you. Today or any day. You're wasting your time."

His eyes narrowed. "What are you! Some sort of jailer?"

"Of course not!" Sally glared at him. "You've tried bullying me. I won't have you bullying her."

He said tightly, "I have no intention of bullying her. I just want to talk things over rationally –"

"Huh! Like you did with me, I suppose. Oh no, Mr Dewer. Try your bulldozer tactics on somebody else. You are not going to see my grandma."

Nick drew himself up to his full height and slammed his clenched fist on the top of the gate, making Sally jump.

"Now look here, Sally Penrose. You can't lead other people's lives for them. If I want to talk to your grandmother, I will."

"And if she doesn't want to see you, she won't!"

Nick met her defiant stare for a long moment, then he let out his breath in a sigh.

"Very well. If that's how it is." With a shrug, he

turned and went back to his car.

Sally blinked in disbelief. Surely he hadn't given up? That wasn't his way. He always got what he wanted.

She stood thoughtfully at the gate, watching him drive away, then she went slowly into the house. He was up to something. But what?

Her grandmother had retreated to the kitchen as usual.

"He's gone, Grandma. But I don't trust him. I think he'll come back," She glanced around uncertainly. "Perhaps I'd better stay in this evening."

Her grandmother frowned. "You promised Jake you'd go to the dance. You can't let him down at the last minute."

"But I can't leave you. What if Nick comes?"

"He won't." Mrs Penrose spread her hand and counted the points off on her fingers. "He doesn't know you'll be out. He's unlikely to come back today, now you've seen him off. He wouldn't come after dark. And I'll lock all the doors and windows as soon as you've gone, so he won't be able to get in anyway."

Sally wasn't really convinced. "Are you sure, Grandma?"

"Of course, dear. We've never had any problems before. Don't worry. I'll be quite all right." She smiled. "Besides, I'm longing to see you in your new dress. If you don't go to the dance tonight, it might be ages before you wear it."

The only mirror in the house was in Sally's bedroom. That evening she stood before it, studying her reflection. Her pale-tangerine dress was flatteringly cut and fitted her slim figure to perfection, the colour giving a glow to her skin. She had piled her fair hair on top of her head, teasing out little tendrils to soften the effect. She put her hand to her bare throat. What jewellery should she wear? Perhaps something simple would be best.

Sally pulled open the top drawer of her dressing-table and took out the tear-drop pearl pendant her grand-mother had given her for her eighteenth birthday. It was antique, and probably had quite a history. But not in her family. Everything had been lost in the fire seven years ago. She hung the pendant round her neck, added the matching ear-rings, and smiled with delight. They were perfect.

Gathering up her bag, she ran lightly down the stairs, waltzed across the lounge and sank in a deep curtsey before her grandmother's chair.

"How do I look, Grandma?"

The old eyes softened with love as they swept over her, lingering at the pendant nesting between her young breasts.

"You look lovely, Sally. Absolutely lovely." There was a catch in her voice as she added, "Young Jake will be bowled over."

Her grandmother had never seen Jake, but she had heard all about him. Sally laughed, remembering how he had gawked at her at the opera last week.

"He'll be feasting his eyes on all the girls."

The Farmers Club dance was being held at The Black Dog and, as usual, Sally would not let Jake pick her up; she was to meet him there. And he certainly feasted his eyes on her as she entered the foyer.

He raised her hand theatrically to his lips. "You're growing lovelier every day."

Sally smiled and touched the lapel of his dinner-jacket. "Moss Bros?" she whispered.

Jake grinned. "The genuine article. It's not only property developers who know how to dress."

She glanced around in alarm. "He's not here, is he?"

"He'd better not be. He's no farmer." Jake tucked her hand in his arm. "We're not going to let thoughts of the enemy ruin our evening."

The hall which The Black Dog hired out for dances was purely functional, with plain cream walls and folding wooden chairs, but it was given a festive air by the colourful dresses of the women, and the shimmering blue jackets of the five-piece band who were playing soft background music.

"Are your parents here?" Sally asked.

Jake nodded. "Dad's on the committee. He'll be opening the dancing."

"Quite an honour." The Trehernes were a jolly couple and Sally usually found them comfortable to be with. "Shall we go and say Hello?"

Jake and Sally had lots of friends, who stopped them for a word or two as they made their way to the far end of the hall. Sally was a bit disconcerted that most people were classing them as a couple, as though there was more between them than their partnership on stage.

His parents greeted her almost as one of the family, and she began to wonder if he too was reading more into their relationship.

Mrs Treherne was complimenting Sally on her dress when, at a signal from the chairman, the drummer beat a tattoo to draw everyone's attention. The evening was about to begin.

There were a few short speeches, then Mr Treherne drew his wife out onto the floor to open the dancing. The rest of the committee followed, and soon others joined in.

Jake watched his parents dance by, then he grinned. "Come on, Sally m'girl. Let's show them how it should be done."

"Such modesty," she laughed as he swept her out onto the floor.

Jake was a good dancer and she had worked with him so often on stage she could follow his lead easily and blend her steps with his. She loved dancing; it gave her a sense of freedom, a oneness with the music flowing in her soul.

As it was traditional to have the first dance, the floor soon became rather crowded and Sally realised that Jake was holding her closer than was really necessary.

She smiled at him. "Opportunist."

He drew her slightly closer. "Of course."

"Give me a chance to breathe," she protested.

His gaze dipped to the deep vee of her neckline. "You're managing very nicely."

Sally laughed. "Jake, you're impossible."

Then she gasped as she caught sight of the tall dark man standing near the door, his black eyes fixed on her.

"Oh no," she breathed.

Jake loosened his hold. "What is it?"

Sally swallowed and managed to say, "Look who's just come in."

With a bit of fancy footwork, Jake swung her round so he could see.

"Nicholas Dewer! What the devil is he doing here!"

Eight

Sally didn't say anything. Her shock on seeing Nick was tinged with relief. If he was here, he couldn't be at home badgering her grandmother.

Jake frowned. "I don't like the way he's glaring at us."

She knew he wasn't glaring at Jake, his intense gaze was meant for her alone. "We're leading the campaign against him. You can't expect him to be pleased to see us."

"He shouldn't have come then." Jake glanced around. "This is a members only do. I'd like to know who had the gall to invite him."

Sally was wondering the same thing. This wasn't only a dance, it was an important social occasion and much business was discussed along with the usual farming gossip. Why would a farmer invite a property developer?

"We're not going to let him spoil our evening," Jake said. "Come on, Sally m'girl, let's give it a whirl." He swung her round and headed for the opposite side of the hall.

Over his shoulder, Sally could still see Nick watching them and she knew that her evening was spoiled already. He wouldn't miss the opportunity to get at her.

But she wasn't going to make it easy for him. She kept Jake dancing for as long as she could, but eventually they had to take a break.

"I'll get you a drink," Jake said. "The usual?"

"Thanks."

While he went to the bar, Sally gazed idly around, and her eyes were drawn instinctively to Nicholas Dewer. He

101

was immaculate, as always, dancing with Gillian, who looked stunning in a slinky low-cut black dress, with diamonds sparkling at her ears and throat, her lovely auburn hair piled high on her head. They made a beautiful couple, moving in perfect coordination as though they were made for one another.

Nick's eyes turned to Sally, and she quickly looked away.

"Your drink," Jake said.

Sally gave him a dazzling smile. "Thank you. It's just what I need." She took a sip of her cider. "Mmm, this is good."

"The real stuff from a cask." Jake scanned the dance-floor as he took a long drink from his glass. "I wonder what he's doing here."

A masculine voice beside him said, "Dancing with the best-looking woman in the place." It was Larry, the young reporter on the *Gazette*. Anita was with him. She smoothed her hand sexily over the hip of her scarlet dress, and he hastily added, "Present company excepted, of course."

"Of course," Anita murmured. She glanced slyly at Gillian Masters and said in a low tone, "She's sharing his suite at The White Hart."

Sally looked down into her glass, she didn't want to talk about Nick's private life.

"Someone said she's his sister," Jake mused.

Larry smirked. "He'd have to say that, wouldn't he."

"Huh!" Anita snorted. "If you believe that, you'll believe anything." She turned eagerly to Sally. "Have you seen her necklace? It's fabulous. D'you think it's real?"

"I expect so." She couldn't imagine Nick tolerating imitations.

"Diamonds," Anita breathed. "What would I do for a necklace like that...."

Larry looked her over speculatively. "Tell me, Anita. What would you do?"

She put her tongue out at him.

Jake said, "Any idea what Dewer's going to do next, Larry? About The Duke's, I mean."

"Dunno. Depends what else Sally's got up her sleeve."

She almost choked on her drink. Surely he couldn't know....

But Larry was grinning at her. "Gave me a nice bit of copy, that meeting. Never seen anything like it."

He obviously thought Sally had made the petition. She wasn't going to enlighten him; she didn't want him trying to interview her grandmother.

Anita asked, "Have you interviewed Mr Dewer, Larry?"

"Not yet. He always palms me off on one of his minions." Larry was watching the dance-floor, the light of battle in his eyes. "But he can't dance all night. He'll have to take a break sometime."

Anita pouted. "Does that mean you're going to spend the whole evening in the bar? This is supposed to be a dance, you know."

"And I'm on a job, ducky." He drained his glass, and put out his hand to her. "OK. Duty before pleasure."

"Charming!" Anita retorted, but she gave Sally a triumphant wink as she led Larry away.

Jake watched them go. "You're very quiet, Sally."

She said evasively, "It's difficult to get a word in when Anita's in good form."

Jake was still watching them. "I wonder why she's set her sights on Larry. He's far too serious. Not her type at all."

No, but you are, Sally thought and wondered why she hadn't noticed it before. "Perhaps she's hoping he'll lead her to the millionaire she's looking for."

"Not much chance of that, when he can't even get an interview." Jake lowered his voice. "Talk of the Devil. Here he comes."

Sally stiffened and glanced around in alarm, but there was no way to escape.

Jake's eyes narrowed shrewdly. "Has he been getting at you, Sally?"

She bit her lip, uncertain how to reply. She couldn't lie to Jake, but she couldn't tell him either. Before she could say anything, Nick was there.

He nodded formally. "Good evening, Treherne. Miss Penrose."

So he was still furious with her. Sally smiled sweetly. "Good evening, Mr Dewer. I didn't know you were a farmer."

"My interests are fairly wide, but they do not include farming." He put his arm round Gillian's waist and drew her forward. "We were invited, as no doubt your news-hound friend was too."

He must have been keeping an eye on them and waited till Larry had gone. Sally took a step closer to Jake for his protection. Nick couldn't bully her in the presence of witnesses.

She said lightly, "Hallo, Gillian. I hope you're not too bored with us yokels."

Gillian smiled. "I'd hardly call you –" She flicked a glance at Jake, "– either of you, yokels. Everyone's very charming. I'm really enjoying myself."

Nick said, "I'll get you a drink, Gill. What'll it be?"

She looked at the large glasses Sally and Jake were holding. "As we're settling in Cornwall, we'd better get to know the customs. I'll have cider, please."

"I'm sure you'll like it," Jake said. "It's very refreshing."

Sally knew he wanted to ask who had invited them to

the dance but, when Nick had gone to the bar, he asked instead, "Have you found a house yet?"

Gillian nodded. "Nick's very single-minded. When he wants something, he goes all out for it."

"Bulldozer tactics," Sally murmured.

Jake asked, "Is it far from town?"

Gillian put her finger to her lips. "I'm not allowed to say. You two have given Nick more than enough trouble over property –"

"Only the theatre," Sally put in.

"The opposition over that has really surprised Nick. I suppose it's because he's so practical he can't understand sentiment." Gillian winced. "He was absolutely livid after that meeting on Thursday. And he said some very uncomplimentary things about you, Sally."

"It was mutual."

Gillian looked sternly at each of them. "We don't want to ruin a pleasant evening. Let's lay off that subject, shall we?"

Sally and Jake exchanged glances. "OK. We'll call a truce."

Nick came over and handed a glass to Gillian. She smelt the cider delicately, tasted it, then looked up in surprise. "Oh, I expected it to be fizzy."

"It's the real thing from a cask," Jake said. "Do you like it?"

She took another sip. "Mmm, I think so. This is one tradition I can take on board." She snapped her fingers. "Talking of traditions, I've just remembered. Tom was telling me about something you said, Sally. You called Nick, Dewer the Devil."

"She put it on a placard too," Nick said wryly.

Sally nodded. "Dewer is the Devil in the folklore of Dartmoor."

Gillian smiled. "Good thing we're this side of the Tamar. You're Devil enough as it is, Nick. What's the story, Sally?"

"Oh, there are several." Sally glanced round the brightly-lit room. "They should really be told out on the lonely moor at dusk."

"We can pretend," Gillian said. "Do tell."

Sally spoke slowly with feeling. "Think of the Devil's hand on a wood in the middle of Dartmoor. Twisting and stunting the trees into hideous shapes. It's called Wistmans Wood. That means bogeyman, or Devil's wood."

She lowered her voice. "At the dead of night, there is the sound of a huntsman's horn and the baying of hounds. Bursting out of the wood comes Dewer the Devil, dressed all in black, astride his headless black horse. Hard upon his heels race the Wisht hounds. Black spectral dogs with gleaming red eyes."

Nick sneered. *"The Hound of the Baskervilles."*

Sally jerked her head, the thread of her narrative broken. "That's Squire Cabell of Buckfastleigh. It's a different legend."

"Shut up, Nick," Gillian said. "You're ruining the story. Do go on, Sally."

She took a sip from her glass of cider and her blue eyes became unfocussed as she lost herself in the legend.

"The Wisht hounds are the souls of unbaptised babies. They roam the moor at night, seeking others to join their pack. Across the moor they race, up rocky tors, down deep river valleys, across quaking bogs. On and on they race until they reach the south-west corner.

"And there stands the Dewerstone, a mighty outcrop of granite with sheer cliffs falling to the river below. This is the domain of Dewer the Devil.

"People keep clear of it at night for Dewer guards it with

his dogs. Lashing his horsewhip, he pursues intruders to the highest crags and hurls them over to crash on the rocks below. Then he takes their souls to his own."

Nobody spoke when she had finished. They stood spellbound, watching her.

Sally blinked, then said softly, "That is the story of Dewer the Devil."

"You're a born storyteller, Sally," Gillian said. "Where did you learn these legends?"

"I was brought up on them. My grandma is an expert on folklore and local history."

Gillian glanced around. "Is she here? I'd love to meet her."

Sally looked Nick straight in the eye. "Grandma doesn't come to dances."

Jake's eyebrows rose at her firm tone. She shrugged and turned to him. "Mr Dewer has discovered that it was Grandma who made the petition."

Gillian wagged her finger. "We're not talking about that. Going back to your story, Sally. Where is this Dewerstone?"

"On the edge of Dartmoor." She paused to consider. "About ten kilometres north of Plymouth. It's on National Trust property, very easy to get to."

"That close." Gillian put her hand on Nick's arm. "You must go and see it, Nick. Meet your ancestor."

"Huh! Fairy stories," he scoffed.

"Oh well, if you're going to be stuffy...." She dropped her hand from his arm and turned to Jake with a dazzling smile. "You're not stuffy, are you Jake? Let's go and dance."

Jake gulped and blushed to the roots of his hair. "Er – yes, of course, Mrs – er – Gillian."

She took his hand and led him to the dance-floor.

As soon as they had gone, Nick said, "OK, Sally. Let's have it straight. Your grandmother didn't come tonight because she knew I'd be here."

Sally threw back her head. "Modesty's not one of your strong points, is it! Of course she didn't know you'd be here. I didn't know either. I told you, Grandma doesn't come to dances."

"Why not?" He glanced towards the end of the hall where clusters of chairs were occupied by gossiping farmfolk. "She doesn't have to dance. There are plenty of middle-aged and elderly people to talk to."

Sally said firmly, "Grandma never goes out."

Nick frowned. "When I came to your house, you said she doesn't receive visitors. Are you ashamed of her, or something?"

"How dare you!" Sally's voice was icy with fury. "My grandmother is the finest woman in the world. She's worth ten of you."

"Why doesn't she see people then?"

He seemed genuinely perplexed and Sally knew she would have to tell him. She glanced around to make sure there was no one within earshot. "You've seen her, Nick."

"Yes, and she looked perfectly normal to me." He paused. "Though I obviously frightened the life out of her."

"Her face, Nick. You saw the scars on her face."

He blinked. "Yes, but –"

Sally leaned forward, her voice low and earnest. "You don't know what it's like for her. Oh, I daresay people stop and stare at you because you're so gorgeous –"

His lips curved in a smile, but before he could speak, she went on.

"But can you imagine what it's like to be pointed at, to have people cringe at the sight of you? To be spurned by all your friends. Some were physically sick when they saw what had happened to her face."

Sally's eyes contracted with pain. "That's why we live in the middle of nowhere. She had to have somewhere to hide. But even here, she isn't accepted. The villagers are afraid of her. They think she's a witch."

Sally pressed her clenched hand to her lips. "I've never told anyone, Nick. Please...."

"It's all right," he said softly. "What happened?"

"It was the fire," she breathed.

"When was this?"

"Seven years ago."

"And she hasn't been out since?"

"She can't." Sally gazed up at him in an appeal for understanding. "I'm all she has, Nick. I must protect her."

He said incredulously, "She hasn't seen anyone in all that time?"

Sally shook her head.

"But that's unhealthy."

"Of course it isn't." Sally drew back indignantly. He didn't understand at all. "We lead a very healthy life, working on the land –"

Nick sighed and said gently, "I'm sure you do. Now don't upset yourself, Sally. You're very young to carry such a burden."

"She's not a burden! I love my grandma!"

"I can see that." Nick glanced up and his tone suddenly brightened. "Come on, Sally, we'd better dance."

"Why? I mean –" She didn't want to be held in his arms, he was far too disturbing at close quarters.

"Here come the sex-pot and the news-hound. We don't want to be caught by them."

Sally had to smile at his description of Anita and Larry. But she didn't want to be cross-examined by Larry, especially not now. The lesser of the two evils was to dance with Nick. She gave him her hand and let him lead her to the dance-floor.When he drew her into his arms, his magnetism began to weave its usual spell. The feel of his hands upon her, the scent of his aftershave, the nearness of him, sent her pulse-rate soaring, making her want to melt against him. But she had to resist. She held herself slightly apart, keeping a definite space between them.

Nick said softly, "There's no need to be afraid of me, Sally."

"I'm not," she murmured. It was her own reaction to him that she was afraid of.

He was a good dancer and she found him easy to follow. They made a circuit of the floor before he spoke again.

"When we were talking earlier, you made no mention of your parents."

She closed her eyes as a wave of pain washed over her. "I – they –" she stammered.

"The fire?" Nick prompted.

She nodded dumbly.

"I'm sorry," he said. "I didn't mean to hurt you. I should have guessed."

She swallowed. "Are your parents – er –?"

He smiled. "My mother is very much alive, queening it in St John's Wood. Running everyone's life for them, if she gets the chance." He shrugged. "I can't remember my father. He walked out when I was two years old."

"Oh, I'm sorry."

Nick looked down into her troubled eyes. "There's no need to be. It was a long time ago." His mouth twisted cynically. "It happens all the time."

That was what had made him so hard, she thought. "You don't have much of an opinion of marriage."

"A mug's game," he snorted. "Look what it's done for

Gillian."

Sally turned her head to glance at Gillian, who was still dancing with Jake. He had lost his shyness of her and they were both smiling as though sharing a good joke.

"She looks happy enough."

Nick said thoughtfully, "Young Treherne seems to be enjoying himself."

Sally laughed. "Jake's in his element. He always has an eye for a pretty girl. Or in this case, a beautiful woman."

"A beautiful woman," Nick repeated softly and the timbre of his voice made Sally's breath catch in her throat. While they had been talking, he had gradually drawn her closer and she was almost moulded to him as they continued to dance, moving as one in time with the music. She dare not meet his eyes. She fixed her gaze on his black bow-tie, but she was very much aware of his chin brushing her temple, his breath lightly fanning her hair.

Halfway down the hall were glass doors leading to a covered terrace. When they reached that point, Nick slid his arm round her waist and whisked her out to the terrace, away from the light streaming through the glass doors and into the deepest shadow.

"You're so beautiful, you're driving me crazy," he murmured, then his lips were upon hers.

Sally knew this was what she had been waiting for, like a drug that has been denied too long. She slid her arms round his neck and clung to him as the kiss deepened with passion. A warmth pervaded her limbs, drawing a primitive longing from deep within her.

"Sally," he murmured, kissing her eyes, her cheek, her neck, then claiming her mouth again. She ran her fingers into his hair, holding him to her, wanting the kiss to go on and on.

Suddenly a sound jarred on her consciousness. The

glass doors had opened as another couple came onto the terrace, letting out a burst of music from the ballroom. From the dance!

Sally put her hands on Nick's shoulders to push him away.

"What about Gillian?" she whispered in alarm.

Nick drew in a deep breath. "It's Treherne you're worried about." He slid his hand down to the tear-drop pearl pendant nestling between her breasts and tugged it, the chain biting into her neck. "Did he give you this?"

"No!" she gasped. "It was Grandma. She gave it to me for my birthday."

Nick held the pendant for a moment and Sally knew that he had given Gillian that fabulous diamond necklace and she flushed with shame. She had been kissing him and letting him kiss her, when he had already bought Gillian's favours. Did he think every woman had her price?

Nick gently replaced the pendant, letting the back of his fingers rest on her skin, then slid his hand down to cup her breast.

"He's not for you, Sally. You're mine."

"No." His hand was far too disturbing, she pushed it away. "You can't buy me, Nick."

"I wouldn't try." His hands were at her waist, trying to draw her to him. "Save the last dance for me, Sally. Let me take you home."

She stood stiffly away. "I'm Jake's partner. He has that right."

"You can't let that boy make love to you. Not after –" He jerked her forward and plundered her mouth, making her senses reel.

But she knew she had to resist. "No. There are certain rules of etiquette –"

"Etiquette!" he snorted. "You're fooling yourself, Sally

Penrose. There could be something wonderful between us. And one day you'll have the courage to admit it."

"Never," she breathed. "I won't give in to you."

His black eyes bored into her for a moment, then he took out a white handkerchief and rubbed it across his mouth and, without another word, turned on his heel and strode back into the ballroom.

Sally stared after him, aghast at the havoc he could wreak within her. She put her fingers tentatively to her lips, bruised by the brand of his kiss, knowing that what he said was true. There was magic between them. But it was purely physical. She wasn't going to degrade herself by giving in to his ego and having an affair with him.

Lifting her head proudly, she went to the cloakroom to repair her make-up, then returned to the ballroom, determined to show Nick that she could stand up to him.

She danced with Jake, with Larry, with several of their friends, and once with Mr Treherne, smiling and exchanging light banter with them. But it was all superficial. She was conscious the whole time of Nick.

Although she resolved not to look at him, she couldn't help noticing that he had no shortage of partners and was surprised that he knew so many people in the farming community.

"Take your partners for the last waltz."

Sally glanced across the room and met piercing black eyes which tried to claim her. She shook her head and turned to Jake with a smile.

"All good things must come to an end."

Jake glanced at his watch. "Good thing summertime ends tonight and we get an extra hour. I've got to be up for the milking."

"You're so romantic," Sally murmured. And they both laughed.

The lights were turned low, the waltz became dreamy, and Sally let Jake hold her smoochily close. She didn't want Nick to suspect that Jake wouldn't be taking her home.

After the dance, she waited in the foyer while Jake fetched her coat and, seeing Nick out of the corner of her eye, touched her fingers intimately to Jake's hand as he put her coat round her shoulders.

His parents had tactfully left early, leaving him the Volvo. Sally slipped her hand through his arm as he walked her across the carpark to her car. She glanced around surreptitiously. There was no sign of the Porsche, so she no longer had to play up.

She kissed Jake lightly, thanked him for a delightful evening, and got into her car.

"I'll follow you out," he said, walking across to the Volvo.

As they emerged from the carpark, he gave her a cheery wave and turned right towards his home. Sally turned left. Her route went past the front of The Black Dog and she was horrified to see the black Porsche standing on the forecourt.

Nick was getting into the car. He glanced up as she drove past, and Sally prayed that he was dazzled by her headlights and couldn't see that she was alone.

Nine

Sally was thoughtful as she worked in the garden next morning. She had always been open with her grandmother but now there was much she couldn't tell her and she knew her description of the dance had been rather sketchy.

But how could she talk about things she didn't fully understand herself? Her feelings for Nick. She hated him for what he represented, the destruction of the traditions she held dear, yet she found his personal magnetism very hard to resist. She couldn't forget his kisses.

Or his anger over the petition to save The Duke's Theatre.

Last night they had agreed not to talk about that. But what were his plans? What was he going to do next? At least she had made it clear that there was no point in coming to try to browbeat her grandmother.

All that day, and the next, Sally chewed over the possibilities. Tuesday was market day and she went into town, eager to find out what was going on.

She took honey to the health-food stall as usual, and, when all the merchandise had been put on display, she set off to do her own shopping. Although she and her grandmother grew most of their fruit and vegetables, they kept no animals, so she was glad to be able to buy really fresh eggs and farmhouse cheese in the market.

She knew many of the stall-holders and exchanged a word here and there as she passed among the stalls, but she was unusually conscious of the shoppers milling about. Her eye was caught by a tall figure, a dark head, the way a man moved. When someone brushed against her arm, she jerked round – to meet the eyes of a stranger. And she knew she was instinctively looking for Nick.

But there was no sign of him.

And why should there be? He wouldn't take time off to come to the market. He was no doubt in his office plotting how to get round the regulations so he could go ahead with his plans.

When she had finished her shopping, Sally walked along Fore Street to see how the demolition was progressing. The gate in the hoardings was open and she was amazed to see how far they had got. The shops had been completely gutted, everything removable had been removed; the doors, windows, roof tiles, even the granite lintels. Only parts of the walls with crumbling plaster remained.

Sally stared at a gaping hole where a fireplace had been wrenched out. Was that what Nick wanted to do to the theatre, tear the heart out of it?

Never! She must stop him before he destroyed everything. She ran along to the theatre to make sure it was still standing.

And it was there, the solid granite building, weathered by time but, as yet, untouched by progress.

That's how it's going to stay, she vowed. No matter what it entailed, she would save the theatre. If only she knew what Nick was going to do now.

She tried to think if there was anyone she could ask, but he was unlikely to discuss his plans with anyone she knew, and there was no point in trying to pick up gossip; it was invariably wrong.

Sally wandered back to her car. She would just have to

wait and see. And be prepared for anything.

But she was not prepared for the sight which met her eyes as she turned the last corner on her way home. There was a black Porsche parked in the lane!

Nick! And he wasn't in the car!

She clenched her teeth in fury. So that was what he had been planning! To come and bully her grandmother behind her back.

Sally drove furiously into the garage and leapt out of the car, slamming the door behind her. Of all the rotten low-down tricks. He knew she went to market on Tuesdays.

She stalked into the house and flung open the kitchen door.

But the room was empty. Fear clutched at her throat. Where was Grandma? What had happened?

Then she heard her grandmother's voice.

Sally swung round. Grandma was in the lounge. And she sounded quite calm. But she couldn't be, not if Nick was there. She must be frightened to death.

Sally strode across the kitchen and wrenched open the door. Her anger boiled over when she saw Nick sitting in *her* armchair, his long legs stretched out casually across the carpet as though he belonged there.

"What the hell are you doing here!"

Her grandmother jerked round, a tentative smile on her lips. "Oh, there you are Sally. I was just telling Nick you'd be back soon."

"Nick?" Sally breathed in disbelief at this familiarity. She moved to stand beside her grandmother's chair, her eyes fixed on his face.

"What are you doing here?"

He smiled suavely. "I *was* having an interesting discussion with your grandmother."

"Discussion! Huh! You don't know the meaning of the

word! I told you not to come and bully her. How dare you
sneak in behind my back!"

Nick uncrossed his legs and sat up straight, his eyes
narrowing dangerously. "I never sneak anywhere. I tele-
phoned your grandmother –"

Sally swung to face her. "Grandma! You never invited
him!"

Her grandmother sighed. "Since we had already met...."

Sally's eyes widened in alarm. "But you can't withdraw
your petition!"

Mrs Penrose lifted her chin. "I have no intention of
doing so. That's not what we were talking about. Well, we
did mention it but –" She waved her hand uncertainly.
"Close the door, Sally. It's rather draughty. And do sit
down instead of hovering like that."

In her haste, Sally had left all the doors open. She went
obediently to close them, her mind in turmoil. What on
earth was going on? Nobody had ever come to the house,
yet her grandmother was calmly chatting to Nick as
though she had visitors every day, and she wasn't covering
her face. He must have been very persuasive to get through
her defences.

And Sally had the uncomfortable feeling that somehow
the two of them were ganging up on her. But that was
impossible, her grandmother was always on her side.

As they never had visitors, there were only two armchairs in the lounge, so Sally drew a chair away from the
dining-table and sat beside her grandmother.

"Well," she demanded. "What did you come for?"

Nick met her belligerent gaze quite steadily. "After
what you told me at the dance –"

Sally's jaw tightened indignantly. "That was in confidence. You had no right –"

"I had every right." He glanced towards Mrs Penrose,

who was silently watching them. "I wanted to talk to your grandmother, but there was no hope of that with you acting as watchdog."

"Just as I said. Sneaking in behind my back."

He jabbed his finger at her. "Now look here, Sally Penrose. You've called me all sorts of names –"

"What do you expect! Coming here determined to destroy everything."

"You know that's not true. The development I'm working on will bring more life to the town."

"Destroying its soul," she snapped. "Pulling down our theatre."

Nick snorted. "You're so steeped in theatricals, you can't tell fact from fiction. Those stories you told on Saturday."

Sally leapt to her feet, but at her grandmother's "Tut, tut," hastily dropped back onto her chair.

"And you're so practical, you can't recognise a good legend when you hear it!"

"You and your Dewerstone," he sneered. "Some jumped up lump of granite on top of a tor."

"It's nothing of the sort! If you'd ever seen it –"

"All right. Show me," he challenged.

She lifted her chin. "Very well, I will."

Nick rose to his feet.

"Not now," she protested, her gaze sweeping over his immaculate dark-grey suit. "It's rough country. You're not dressed for it."

"I didn't mean now." He glanced at his watch. "I have a meeting in forty minutes. And another tomorrow morning. I'll pick you up – say one o'clock? Does that give enough time to get back to the car before dark?"

"Easily. It's only about a kilometre from the carpark, and even you should be able to manage that in less than an hour."

He ignored her taunt, and put out his hand to her grandmother. "It's been a pleasure talking to you, Mrs Penrose."

She shook his hand. "I'm glad to have met you Nick. Sally will see you out. By the front door," she added as Sally turned towards the kitchen.

Sally walked briskly to the door and ushered Nick out into the hall. Before she could reach for the front door lock, he caught her hand.

"Let me go!" she hissed.

He pulled her round and pointed at the lovely old staircase hewn from solid oak. "If you must preserve old buildings, choose one with a feature like that. Not a tumbledown wreck of a theatre."

"It's not a wreck," she protested. "And you're not going to pull it down."

"We'll see." He turned to open the front door. "Be ready at one tomorrow." And with that, he walked out, closing the door behind him.

Sally threw the bolts, then went thoughtfully back into the lounge. She still couldn't credit that her grandmother had willingly let Nick into the house.

"Just what did he come for, Grandma? Has he been bullying you?"

"Not at all." Mrs Penrose was carrying the chair to the dining-alcove. She put it in place and stood with her hand on the back of it. "We talked about the theatre, of course. But he was asking about the folklore concerning his name."

Sally frowned. "You mean Wistmans Wood and the Dewerstone?"

"That's right." Mrs Penrose turned, and Sally was surprised to see her eyes bright with amusement. "He asked if I would show him the Dewerstone, but I told him I'm not agile enough. You'd be a much better guide."

Sally stared. "You mean – !"

Her grandmother smiled. "He set you a trap, Sally, and you walked straight into it."

Sally drew in her breath. "Of all the devious, conniving –" She glared at the window, but the Porsche was no longer outside the gate. "He can go on his own! I'm not taking him."

"Yes you are, dear," her grandmother said firmly. "You've given your word. Besides, if you can get him interested in our heritage, he might begin to understand why we want to save The Duke's."

The weather forecast was good, but Sally knew better than to trust it. She put on her waterproof anorak over her cherry-red track-suit, and decided to wear trainers to give flexibility on the rough ground.

A few minutes to one, she kissed her grandmother goodbye and ran lightly down the drive, reaching the gate just as the Porsche drew up outside.

Nick leaned over and opened the passenger door for her. "Right on time."

"Stage training," she said, settling into the seat and fastening her seat-belt. Nick was wearing blue jeans and a forest-green weatherproof jacket.

"I see you're going incognito."

He raised one eyebrow. "How do you mean?"

"This is the first time I've seen you not wearing black or dark-grey."

He laughed. "What did you expect? A black jump-suit with horns and a tail."

"No trident?" she asked, determined to keep the tone light. She may have been tricked into this trip, but it was a fine November day and she wasn't one to bear a grudge.

The black car took them smoothly through Cornwall, then down to the narrow granite bridge over the Tamar and up into Devon. Soon they were driving across the edge of Dartmoor, with exhilarating views of the bracken and coarse-grass covered slopes, a slight haze throwing into relief the distant tors, each with a craggy granite outcrop on top.

Sally leaned forward. "Next turning on the left."

Nick slowed the car. "There's no signpost."

"We don't need one."

The road was narrow and winding, and seemed to be leading nowhere.

Nick asked wryly, "Are we being pisky-led?"

"Of course not," Sally retorted. "There are no piskies in Devon. They're pixies."

He put his hand on her knee. "But I've brought a Cornish pisky with me."

The touch of his hand made her suddenly far more aware of him and she flushed, remembering the way he had held her and kissed her at the dance on Saturday. She swallowed and risked a glance at his face, but he was watching the road. He lifted his hand to the wheel again, quite unaware of her reaction.

They passed through a village, then once again the road was narrow and winding, dropping down into a wooded valley.

"The carpark's on the left, just over the bridge," Sally said.

"Oh really," Nick retorted sceptically and she was sure he thought they were lost.

But it was there, as she had known, and to her chagrin there were three cars and a minibus parked in the clearing. No matter what time you came, there were always cars parked, she thought, but the wilderness was so large there was no need to meet anyone.

Nick drew up and parked beside one of the granite buttresses, which were remains of old china-clay works, but Sally did not explain. He might decide to demolish them and build a teashop or something equally unsuitable!

Nick took a packet of fudge from the shelf and slipped it into his pocket before locking the car.

"Emergency rations. I don't trust these piskies."

"It's the Devil you have to be wary of here." She saw that he had heeded her warning of rough country and was wearing trainers. "This way." She set off towards the river.

Nick looked around disparagingly at the modern wooden footbridge and the noticeboard beyond.

"A tourist attraction," he sneered

"Such is infamy." Sally smiled to herself; he was in for a surprise.

They paused on the bridge to gaze down into the swift-flowing river, its clear waters boiling and splashing over the rocks.

"It gets a bit wilder further up," she said.

Nick waved his hand towards the rock-strewn hillside visible through the trees. "I assume everything does."

The path, an ancient track from long-disused workings on the far side of the hill, was wide enough for them to walk side by side. They made their way steadily upwards, marvelling at the ruggedness of the hill, which seemed to be composed of monstrous granite boulders piled haphazard upon one another.

"The hand of the Devil," Sally murmured ominously.

"Ah, but softened by nature," Nick said. Oaks, a few birch trees and hollies were growing on top of the moss-covered rocks, their roots clinging to the sides of the boulders.

"But only the Devil would plant trees on top of the

rocks," Sally persisted. "Anyone else would have planted them in the hollows."

"They probably are hollows, with no soil."

"There must be some." She pointed to a couple of molehills beside the path.

Nick laughed. "I thought I was the practical one with no soul." He looked up at a rocky rampart visible between the tree trunks. "Is that your Dewerstone?"

Sally put her hand to her chin and pretended to consider. "It's some years since I was last here, but no, I don't think it is."

They walked on for a while, then she hesitated. "We're getting a long way from the river. Look there's a path going down. Shall we go that way?"

Nick shrugged. "You're the guide."

The lower path was narrow so they had to go in single file. Sally skipped happily along, the low sun through the bare trees touching her hair with gold. She loved this rugged wilderness, and the fact that she was stringing Nick along added spice to the day.

The path wound lower, round a rocky buttress and, at a corner, Sally stopped dead, slapping her hand to her mouth.

"What's the matter?" Nick asked anxiously, hurrying down to her. Then he caught his breath in amazement. "Wow!"

They were looking straight across the face of a vertical cliff. It stretched high above them, breaking off in an overhang just below their level, then falling sheer another fifteen metres to a boulder-strewn plateau above the river bank.

Sally turned to Nick, her blue eyes sparkling with delight. "The Dewerstone, Mr Dewer."

"Fantastic," he breathed. "I never expected anything

like this. It's – well – it's awe-inspiring."

She peered down at the mossy rocks in the shady depths below. "I don't think the sun ever gets down there."

Nick couldn't take his eyes off the rock. "A sheer cliff in the middle of nowhere. And stunted trees growing out of bare rock. No wonder it's called the Devil's stone."

"It's a good legend," Sally said, hoping that he would now begin to understand.

But his gaze had become speculative. "It must be – what? Forty, fifty metres high. And all those convenient fissures. It'd be good for rock climbing."

"Barbarism," Sally said. Seeing the minibus in the carpark, she had expected the cliff to be swarming with climbers. "I'd much rather see it as nature intended. It's far more impressive."

"It's impressive all right," he agreed, but she knew he was only thinking how it could be used.

He peered at the path ahead. "It's a bit steep. I'll go first."

She knew that steps had been made so it wasn't danger-ous, but she stood aside, letting him go in front, then slowly followed his tall figure down. They were poles apart, she thought despairingly. If he couldn't appreciate the mystery of this place, he would never begin to un-derstand her love for The Duke's Theatre.

Nick was standing motionless, staring up at the cliff. "I'd like to see the top. Is there an easier way up than that?" He indicated a rope hanging down the rock face.

"We can go back the way we came. The old track goes almost to the top." She turned to gaze up river. "There are more cliffs, not so impressive as this. Then there's a rough bit." She tapped her lip thoughtfully. "I scrambled down it once. I suppose we could get up."

"Let's go and see."

The path meandered over rocks and the roots of trees

beside the fast-flowing river. Way ahead Sally could see brightly coloured jackets; an Outward Bound party practising river crossings, she assumed.

Long before she reached them, she stopped and pointed at the rugged hillside, trees growing among moss-covered granite boulders with patches of grass and fallen oakleaves between.

"About here, I think."

"Should be possible," Nick mused. "If you're feeling like a mountain goat. OK. Off you go."

Sally pulled a pair of gloves from her pocket and put them on before scrambling up onto the hillside. Zig-zagging from root to boulder to hollow, she made her way up, the exhilaration of the climb making her glow with happiness.

Up and up she went, until, hooking her arm round a tree trunk, she stood triumphantly at the top, unaware how appealing she looked to the man following closely behind.

"We made it," she laughed.

"Good going," Nick said. He glanced around. "The top of the cliff's back there?"

"Er – yes." She followed him reluctantly among the stunted trees on the crest of the hill until he approached the bare granite mass at the top of the Dewerstone.

Sally grasped his hand. "Please, Nick. Don't go any closer."

He smiled. "It's all right. I just want to have a look."

"No," she begged, fear clutching at her stomach. "You've seen what it's like. It's dangerous. Don't go any nearer."

"Sally," he said evenly. "I've stood on the girders of a ten-story building. I'm not going to do anything stupid."

"Please," she begged.

But he unclasped her fingers from his hand and moved towards the edge.

Panic swept over her. She turned away and wrapped her arms round a tree trunk, closing her eyes tightly. She couldn't bear to look. This was the Devil's stone and the Devil always claimed his own.

She pressed her cheek to the rough trunk of the tree as her eyes pricked with tears. What was he doing? Was he leaning over the edge? It was so quiet she could hear only the slight rustle of dead leaves and her own rasping breath. Then the sudden harsh cry of a jackdaw.

Her heart almost stopped beating. Oh no! Nick was gone! He had fallen over the cliff. Tears spilled freely down her cheeks.

A hand on her shoulder made her jump out of her skin. "It's perfect," Nick said enthusiastically. "I must try climbing here."

Sally sagged with relief. He was all right. He was safe. Then she was suddenly angry. He had deliberately frightened her. She kept her head turned away, she daren't let him see her tears.

"Now you've satisfied your curiosity," she snapped, "perhaps we can go."

But he pulled her round to face him.

"Sally," he breathed, his gaze moving incredulously over her tear-stained face. "I had no idea. I'm sorry." He slid his arm round her shoulders and, taking out a handkerchief, began gently wiping away her tears. "I wasn't in any danger. Really."

"I don't care if you were," she said mutinously, dashing the tears away with the back of her hand. "It's your life, you can throw it away if you want to."

He gazed down into her face for a moment, then he glanced around. "This place is a bit spooky. Let's get out into the sunshine."

Sally jerked away from him and hurried up the hill and

out onto the open moorland beyond. She strode over the close-cropped sheep-pasture to the flat rock at the top and sat down with her back to him. He had seen her at her most vulnerable and she couldn't forgive him for that.

Nick sat down a short distance away, without a word. She tried to ignore him but she was very conscious of his lithe figure, leaning slightly forward as he studied the panoramic view below.

After a while he opened the packet of fudge from his pocket and offered it to her. She took a piece, accepting it as his way of bridging the constraint between them.

"I thought Dartmoor was open scrubland," he said. "Not woods and neat pasture like this."

"You're looking the wrong way." She jerked her thumb over her shoulder. "Dartmoor's over there."

"Be a pity not to take a look, now we've come this far." He consulted his watch. "It's not yet three. We've plenty of time."

Sally glanced up at the sky. It was beginning to cloud over but there was no danger of rain yet.

"OK." She stepped up onto the rock and waved her right arm. "There are china-clay works over there. If you want it really wild," her arm swung in an arc, "we'll have to go that way."

She looked up at Nick as he joined her on top of the rock. "The way the Devil comes."

He gave a wicked grin. "In that case, we must definitely go that way."

Ten

It was easy going at first, but it got rougher. Sally led the way through bracken, over rocks, up hills, down gullies, round a tor, to show Nick the wildest parts of Dartmoor she could find.

They were on a scrubby hillside dotted with boulders and patches of heather. She clambered down into a hollow and sat on a slab of granite.

"Let's rest for a bit."

Nick dropped onto a boulder beside her. He took the fudge from his pocket and offered her a piece.

"Time's getting on. We'd better start back when we've eaten this."

Sally chewed the fudge slowly. Down in the hollow, they couldn't see any of the surrounding tors.

"We might be anywhere in the world," she mused.

"Not quite." Nick glanced around at the rocks. "You don't get granite like this in many places. You have to choose the right kind for the job."

"Buildings," she said bitterly. "Don't you ever think of anything else?"

He smiled. "Of course. But look, Sally. Men have been building since the year dot. All those hut circles, cairns, standing stones we've seen. They didn't get there by accident."

"I suppose not," she conceded. "And sometimes you can't tell whether stream banks are in their right place or whether they were cut out by the tin miners of old." She looked up at him. "Nothing's really natural, is it? Except the Dewerstone."

"That's natural enough. And we'd better be getting back there."

Sally frowned. "The light's fading early. It must be the overcast sky."

Nick smote his forehead. "And the fact that summertime ended a few days ago! I'd completely forgotten."

She leapt up. "It'll be dark in half an hour. We'd better get to the nearest road."

She scrambled out of the hollow, then stood stock-still, gazing round in bewilderment. The view had completely disappeared. She could see only a few metres of ground in front of her. Everything else was hidden by thick blanketing fog.

The dreaded Dartmoor mist, which crept up on the unwary. Stories of old flashed through her mind, of people getting lost, never to return....

"Low cloud," Nick said in annoyance. "This is going to make it tricky. Well, which way do we go?"

Sally stared at him. "I've no idea."

He said sharply, "But you know where we are!"

"To within two or three kilometres, yes. But –"

"Two or three –! he exclaimed.

"This isn't the middle of town, with signposts on every corner," she retorted.

'But you were taking a definite route."

"Nobody knows Dartmoor that well. I was just heading for the heights." She glanced around, avoiding his eyes. "Besides, I've never been to this part before."

Nick caught hold of her shoulders. "You stupid fool! Why on earth didn't you say? You realise what you've done!"

He dropped his hands from her shoulders and let out

his breath in a sigh. "No. I should have had more sense. Coming out here without a map or compass." He frowned. "We'd better make the most of what's left of the daylight. There must be something to show which way we came."

They studied the ground but could find no footprints, nothing.

Nick straightened up. "We'll go downhill. If this is low cloud, we should come out underneath it."

He set off at a brisk pace over the boulders and heather down the hill. Sally scrambled after him, but soon he was only a vague shape disappearing into the fog.

"Wait!" she yelled. "Wait for me."

Nick glanced over his shoulder, then turned to watch her stumble towards him.

"You're going too fast," she gasped. "Don't leave me behind."

"I'm sorry," he said. "That was almost criminal. You might have fallen." He slid his arm round her waist as she reached him. "I shouldn't take it out on you, Sally. We're both to blame."

"Yes," she panted, too out of breath to argue.

He sat her down on a boulder. "We'll have a short rest, then we'll go carefully, and keep together. All right?"

She nodded dumbly, taking great lungfuls of the cool moist air.

When she had recovered, he handed her a piece of fudge. "Emergency rations to keep up our strength. OK, now on we go."

They continued cautiously down the slope a short way, then came to an abrupt halt. A sheer drop, and through the fog it was impossible to see what was at the bottom.

"What do we do now?" Sally wailed.

"It's plain stupid stumbling about in the fog. We can't go forward, there's no point in going back." Nick peered to either side. "Look, there's a narrow path here."

"Probably a sheep track," Sally said.

"Then it's bound to lead to shelter. We'll have to sit it out till the fog lifts."

Sally gulped. She knew what that meant. They might be stuck out here all night.

"All right," she said. "Lead the way."

She followed him closely along the narrow track which wound across the hillside, through the heather, round the boulders, not letting him get more than a few paces ahead. He looked back frequently to make sure she was there.

Then he stopped and put out his hand to her. "Journey's end. At least, for the time being. Look."

Peering through the fog, she could see a sort of cave. Whether it was natural or man-made was difficult to say.

Nick strode across to the entrance and looked in. "No animals inside. We can shelter here."

Sally hesitated. "It might be a burial place."

"I doubt it." Nick ducked in under the low overhang. "More likely to be a house for piskies, pixies, or whatever the little people here are called."

"You shouldn't joke about them."

"They've already led us a merry dance." He was searching the cave. "Somebody's made a bed of heather. I'm sure no spirits will mind if we make use of it."

Sally gulped. She had no intention of sharing a bed with him!

"Come on," he urged. "It's dry, and far more comfortable to sit on than a granite boulder."

To sit on? That was all right then. She ducked into the cave and found him sitting casually on a heather cushion and leaning back against the rock wall. She sat down a short distance from him. She knew it would get cold as the evening wore on, but she wasn't going to let him get any ideas.

"This heather's comfortable," she said. "I suppose somebody's been camping up here."

"I hope that doesn't mean it's very remote." Nick took the packet of fudge from his pocket. "Emergency rations didn't last long. There's only three bits left."

"As it happens, I had the same idea." She took a paper bag from her pocket and handed it to him. "Barley-sugar."

"Good girl. This'll keep us going. But we'd better ration them. One an hour."

"All right." Sally yawned. Tramping about in the fresh air had made her sleepy.

She settled more comfortably, leaning back against the rock wall and gazing out at the fog. It was an odd situation, she thought. Instead of arguing the merits and demerits of property development, they were sitting in the half-light, in the middle of nowhere, sharing a bag of sweets.

She yawned again. Her eyelids were beginning to droop. She tried to concentrate on watching the fog, looking for anything to keep her awake, but gradually weariness took over. She slid down onto the heather and fell asleep.

She slept restlessly, disturbed by dreams. Then slowly something penetrated her consciousness.

There was a smell in her nostrils, a sound in her ears.

Sally snapped her eyes open. Yellow light. Shadows leaping on the wall. The acrid smell of smoke. The crackle of flames.

Fire!

And suddenly she was back ... back ... back....

Back to that fire seven years ago.

Smoke was billowing in her bedroom window, the curtains were alight. Flames were devouring the staircase outside with a deafening roar. There was the crash of falling timbers, the searing heat, the smoke. The whole house was ablaze. And she was trapped!

The fire was closing in on her, choking, suffocating....

Sally backed away, her eyes dilating with panic. A scream tore from her throat. Then another.

"Grandma!" she screamed. "Save me! Save me!"

Her head turned wildly from side to side, seeking escape. Darkness.

She rushed blindly out into the night, stumbling through the heather, tripping over roots and boulders, until she fell to the ground sobbing loudly like the child she had been.

"Save me! Save me!"

She pressed close to the ground, quivering with fear.

Then strong hands were upon her, lifting her trembling body. She threw her arms round his neck, clinging tightly like a child.

"Save me. Save me," she begged.

"You're all right, Sally," he murmured. "You're quite safe."

She buried her face in his neck, sobbing incoherently. "Grandma, save me...."

Nick carefully eased from a crouch to sit on the ground, lifting her onto his lap. He held her close, gently stroking her hair, her shoulder and down her back, murmuring reassuringly all the time. "It's all right, Sally. You're quite safe."

But her fear ran deep. She clung to him, trembling at the remembered horrors which still held her in thrall.

He continued to stroke and soothe her, and gradually her sobbing eased, her racing pulse began to slow and she became still in his arms, as a feeling of peace seeped into her troubled mind.

Nick glanced over his shoulder. He had thought a small fire would cheer them up! He had made it of dead heather and gorse on a flat stone in front of the cave, and it had burned quickly. Now only a small red glow remained. He daren't stay any longer or that would burn out, then he would have no idea which way to go and might blunder about in the dark for ages.

It was tricky trying to stand up with the girl in his arms and he stumbled as he almost lost his balance. His sudden movement jerked Sally out of her nightmare.

She became aware of soft warmth against her cheek, strong arms enfolding her, and she knew she was safe. There was no fire, no danger.

As he carried her to the cave, her feeling of peace was transformed. The musky scent of his skin, the beat of his heart against her ribs, sent a warm glow through her body.

She trembled as he laid her gently on the bed of heather in the cave and, thinking she was cold, he lay down beside her. Murmuring softly, he continued to stroke her hair, her shoulder and down her back, but her body was moulded to his and the feel of his hands was no longer soothing. She was breathing hard, and so was he.

She felt his lips brush her forehead, her temple, her cheek. Her pulse began to race as she was swept by a deep longing and she turned her head so that her lips met his.

He drew her closer as the kiss deepened with passion, his tongue probing the sweetness of her mouth, making her senses reel.

His hand slid under her anorak to cup her breast. "Sally?" he asked softly.

"Yes," she breathed, knowing there could be no holding back now. She wanted him to make love to her.

But to her dismay, he drew away from her and sat up. Then she heard the rasp of a zip and, by his movements, she realised that he was taking off his jacket.

"Heather's a bit prickly. This'll be more comfortable," he said, spreading his jacket over it.

Then she was in his arms and he was kissing her lips, her eyes, her neck, and tugging aside the top of her track-suit to caress her young breasts.

She smoothed her hands over his shirt, delighting in the hardness of the muscles of his chest and back, his heart pounding in unison with her own.

His kisses became more demanding, making her melt with desire, and she remembered that he thought she was experienced. She had to let him know. As his fingers moved down below her waist, she lightly touched the back of his hand.

"Nick, I've never...."

His hands stilled uncertainly, and she pressed her lips to his throat to tell him that she wasn't stopping him.

'I won't hurt you, Sally," he murmured, his voice husky with desire.

He was very gentle, kissing and caressing her, bringing her need to such a pitch she could hardly bear it.

"Please," she begged.

Then he came to her, and she was filled with such exquisite joy as she had never imagined. It was as though she had never lived until this moment.

And she knew that she loved him.

Later, as she lay contentedly in his arms, Nick gently stroked her cheek.

"Tell me about the fire, Sally."

She buried her face against his chest. "It was terrible. Unbelievably frightening. I've never talked about it. Not to anyone."

"It might help," he said softly.

"There's never been anyone. I mean, Grandma was there. It was worse for her."

"Tell me, Sally."

Held safe in his arms, she knew she could, at last, talk about it.

"We had a big house. Grandma lived with us, Mummy and Daddy and me." She broke off. "It sounds silly calling them that now, but I was only a child then."

"Go on," Nick urged gently.

"My bedroom was on the top floor. I don't know how the fire started. It was the middle of the night. Something must have woken me...."

Hesitantly, in bits and pieces, she told him of the horror of that night, how she had been trapped in her bedroom.

"Grandma saved me. I don't know much about it. All I remember is the utter relief when she came. She wrapped a blanket over me and got me out onto the sloping roof."

Sally gulped. "She was badly burned, Nick. It was the blanket round me that saved the left side of her face. The other side, and her hands...."

"What about you, Sally?"

"I spent some days in hospital. The effect of smoke. There's not a mark on me. But Grandma –"

Sally caught her breath.

"She was a lovely woman. Very popular. She had lots of friends." Sally paused and added in awe, "And she threw it all away for me."

"How do you mean?"

"She had already been rescued by neighbours. They said the fire was so fierce nobody else could possibly have survived. But she went back into the house to find me."

Sally tried to see his face in the darkness. "I owe her my life, Nick. I must protect her."

"Your parents?" he asked softly.

"They were found in bed. The doctor said they had suffocated in their sleep, they didn't suffer any pain."

Nick drew in his breath. "And you've carried that in

your heart all these years."

"I had terrible nightmares at first," she whispered. "But I don't have them very often now."

"Until I foolishly lit a fire to cheer us up!" His arms tightened round her. "You told me your grandmother had been in a fire, but you're so lovely, Sally, it never occurred to me that you were there too." He paused, then added thoughtfully, "That's why there's no fireplace in your lounge."

"I couldn't bear it. The flames...." She sighed and added softly, "But somehow I don't feel so afraid any more. Perhaps telling you has helped to release the memories I've had locked up for so long. Maybe now I can let them go."

"Something good may have come out of my thought-lessness after all," he said softly.

"Don't blame yourself," she murmured. "You couldn't know."

Reliving her nightmare had wearied her and she nestled more comfortably against his chest and drifted to the verge of sleep, happy in the knowledge that she was in the arms of the man she loved.

He shook her awake. "Sally."

"What is it?" she asked sleepily.

"The fog. It's lifting."

She opened her eyes and was surprised to be able to see him silhouetted against a lighter background. She sat up. Moonlight was streaming into the cave.

"Almost full moon," Nick said. "If we go carefully, we should be able to make our way back."

"But it's the middle of the night," she protested.

He laughed. "Would you believe, it's only half past nine."

"Is it?" She glanced at her watch. "We seem to have been

here for hours."

"We have," he said. "About four hours."

Was that all? So much had happened, it seemed a lifetime to her. She stood up stiffly.

"We'd best be on our way before it clouds up again."

Nick handed her half the barley-sugars and she ate one, putting the rest into her pocket as she stepped outside.

"It's beautiful," she breathed, gazing around at the moonlit landscape, with all the colour bleached out of it. The rugged tors were etched against the sky, granite boulders showing white with very black shadows.

Nick pointed. "Lights. There's a house down there. We'll try to go that way." He took her hand. "Be careful. Moonlight's deceptive and we don't want a sprained ankle."

They made their way cautiously down the slope, trying to avoid the boulders, and soon came to a track.

"There must be an old quarry or something further up," Sally said.

Nick shrugged. "Who cares. It's the house at the bottom we want."

It was fairly easy going down the rutted track in the moonlight and in a very short time they reached a small stone cottage.

"What are we going to do?" Sally asked. "I mean, we can't just knock them up."

"We can, and we will," Nick stated.

"But I –" She glanced down at herself, she had no idea how dishevelled she might be. "Do I look all right?"

Nick kissed her lightly on the tip of her nose. "You look perfect. Now, don't worry about a thing."

He stepped forward and knocked on the door. "Travellers who've lost their way," he explained to the man who answered. They talked in low voices, money changed hands, then the man put on a coat and went to the garage to get out his Land Rover.

Soon Nick and Sally were back at the carpark and Nick was unlocking the Porsche.

"Been a long afternoon," he said. "Do you want to stop somewhere for a meal?"

Now they were back in familiar surroundings, Sally was suddenly shy.

"I'd rather go straight home. It's getting late, Grandma might be worried."

It was only an excuse and she wasn't sure whether he believed her, but he did as she asked.

They spoke little as the car cut a swathe through the night and pulled up outside her home.

"Sally?" Nick murmured, and drew her into his arms and kissed her.

She clung to him for a moment, reliving the ecstasy of the cave. Then her eyes widened in alarm. "What am I going to tell Grandma?"

"Do you have to tell her anything?"

"I usually tell her everything – well, almost everything. She never goes out, Nick. She lives through me."

Nick ran his finger lightly down the line of her cheek. "Don't blacken my character too much, will you, Sally."

She smiled. "How can I, Mr Dewer? You're the Devil already."

Then she kissed him lightly on the cheek and slipped out of the car.

Eleven

Her grandmother must have seen the car headlights, she was in the kitchen making cocoa when Sally went in.

"Did you have a good day, dear?"

"Interesting," Sally said, unable to meet her grandmother's eyes. She told in great detail of Nick's reaction to the Dewerstone, but skimmed over their adventure on Dartmoor. She wasn't ready yet to talk about her momentous discovery, the fact that she loved Nick.

That night, as she lay in bed, Sally went over the events of the day, squirming with delight as she recalled his lovemaking. She had been drawn to him the moment she set eyes on him in the theatre. Then when he had kissed her.... No man had ever affected her like that, awakening her to womanhood. She should have known he was the only man for her. She loved him. She would always love him.

Today she had told him things she had never told anyone, baring her innermost soul. And he had been so gentle, so understanding. Surely he must have some feelings for her....

And with that thought, she fell asleep to dream of floating in his arms on a cloud drifting through a moonlit sky.

Cloud cuckoo land, she thought bitterly three days later when there had been no word from him. No phone-call. No message. Nothing.

But what could she expect? She had known all along that he was living with Gillian Masters. He was a sophisticated city man, accustomed to getting what he wanted. And he had made his intentions perfectly clear.

"I want you, Sally Penrose."

She had been able to resist him when she knew she was threatened. But he had bided his time. And when she was at her most vulnerable, she had given in. More than that. She had welcomed him to her, she had wanted him to make love to her.

Oh, he was very clever. He knew exactly how to manipulate her. He had made use of her, and now he had discarded her.

Sally buried her face in her hands. It was too late now. She couldn't hate him for what he was. Out on that hillside she had discovered that she loved him. And it was breaking her heart.

But life had to go on.

There was plenty to do in the garden, tidying up the autumn debris. Sally worked diligently, raking leaves, cutting down the old plants, pruning, digging, anything to keep her busy so her grandma should not suspect how wretched she felt.

On Tuesday morning her spirits rallied. She packed the honey and herbs into her Micra and set off eagerly for town. Nick knew she always went in to market. He was bound to seek her there.

She kept looking for him every step she went. She was so intent on searching for him as she put out the honey on the stall, she let a jar slip through her fingers and it smashed to smithereens on the stone floor.

"There go your profits," the stall-holder said sympathetically. "Sally, you're not usually in such a dither. You all right?"

"Just a bit tired. Have you got something to clear up this mess?"

The extra job kept Sally longer than usual at the market stall, but Nick didn't come. And he wasn't going to come, she decided. If she wanted to seem him, she would have to make the first move.

She hurried through her shopping, stowed it in her car and went to The White Hart.

She hesitated a moment outside the impressive entrance in the hope that he might come out. Then she crossed the foyer to the reception desk.

"I'd like to speak to Mr Dewer, please."

The blonde receptionist looked her over dismissively. "Mr Dewer is not in. Would you care to leave a message?"

Sally shook her head. If he didn't want to see her, there was nothing she could say to him. She wandered disconsolately back to her car.

Driving home, past leafless hedges and bare trees, she couldn't help thinking how desolate the countryside was. And would be all winter. Just as her life would be.

As she turned the final corner, a black car was disappearing up the lane. She only got a glimpse of it, but she was sure it was the Porsche.

Nick! And he had come when he knew she would be out! After all she had told him last week, how dare he come and bully her grandmother!

Sally leapt out of her car and strode furiously into the house. "Grandma! Has he been here?"

Her grandmother turned from the sink. "Who do you mean, dear?"

"Nick, of course."

Mrs Penrose touched nervous fingers to her white hair, drawn back into its customary neat bun. "No, dear. What made you think he had?"

"I saw a car. I – I thought it was the Porsche." So he hadn't come. He didn't want to have anything to do with her any more. She sank onto a chair as a wave of despair swept over her and, dropping her head onto her arms, she burst into tears.

"Oh Sally, my dear. Don't cry." She felt her grandmother's comforting arm round her shoulders.

"You don't understand, Grandma."

Mrs Penrose spoke softly. "I think I do, dear."

Sally lifted her tear-stained face. "I love him, Grandma. I know I shouldn't, but –" She gulped. "Last week, when we were lost on the moor –"

"Don't tell me, Sally. There are some things so private you never talk about them." She smiled with the wisdom of her years. "Besides, there's no need. You were so radiant when you came home, I could guess what had happened."

Sally blinked. "And you weren't shocked?"

"I was young once, dear." She studied her granddaughter thoughtfully. "There was such tension between you...."

"He doesn't want me any more." Sally took out her handkerchief and dabbed at her eyes. "It's nearly a week now, and I haven't heard from him."

"He's a busy man, Sally. Not like us." She glanced round her spotless kitchen. "We don't have to work. It's only for our own health. And at this time of the year, when the bees stay in the hive, we don't really have any responsibilities. But he has plenty. He's chairman of a big company with projects not only here, but Exeter, London...."

"He could have phoned," Sally wailed.

Her grandmother gripped Sally's shoulder reassuringly. "He will, dear. I'm sure of it."

But Sally wasn't at all sure.

As the days dragged by, she couldn't get interested in

anything. Not even the activities of the Dramatic Society.

They were starting rehearsals in earnest for the Edwardian melodrama. Jake was playing the wicked squire. In Act I, he seduced and murdered a young girl, played by Anita. And for the rest of the play, her sister, played by Sally, had to outwit him and bring him to justice.

Sally had learned her part and was word-perfect, but she couldn't summon up any enthusiasm.

As they were going through Act II yet again, she realised what the trouble was. She didn't want to work so closely with Jake. He touched her too often, assuming an intimacy she couldn't allow.

Sue was trying to direct them. "Cut," she called. "Sally, you're just not with it. What's the matter?"

Sally glanced around at the assembled cast, and saw an answer to her problem.

"Quite frankly, I don't think I'm right for this part. I mean, I'm too small and fragile –"

Jake snorted. "You! Fragile!"

"Well, I look fragile," she persisted. "I'm more likely to be murdered by the wicked squire than stand up to him."

Sue studied her for a moment, then looked at the other members of the cast. "OK, Anita. You try it."

Anita's brown eyes lit up with delight. "Sally," she breathed. "You'd give me the lead?"

"You're more suited to it than I am." And more suited to Jake, she thought.

He was a bit put out at first, but soon he and Anita were absorbed in sorting out the action of the play, and Sally was able to sit in the stalls and let her mind wander.

Not that it ever wandered far. She wondered where Nick was, what he was doing, if he ever thought of her. By asking around, she had learned that he hadn't been seen in town all week. Work on demolishing the shops was almost completed, so he hadn't changed his mind about that. Perhaps he was in London with his lawyers, trying to find a way round the regulations. Or maybe he had handed over to one of his subordinates and moved out of town altogether.

Though Sally couldn't imagine him doing that. He had been so sure that his personal intervention would get him permission to demolish the theatre, to tear the heart out of the cultural life of the town, just as he had turned her own life upside down.

Nothing had been the same since he appeared on the scene. Even the close rapport she had with her grand-mother was not so complete. She often found her grand-mother looking thoughtful, even secretive, as she never had before.

Days passed and Sally came to the conclusion that Nick wasn't going to contact her on a personal level again. As she had no intention of giving up the fight to save The Duke's Theatre, she was bound to see him at the planning meetings. Somehow she would have to find the courage to face him when the time came.

Meanwhile she had to go through with her normal duties.

The following Tuesday, she took honey to the market as usual, then did her weekly shopping. She was taking it back to her car, and was halfway across the carpark, when she stopped dead.

Leaning casually against her car, his arms folded across his chest, was Nick!

He straighened up when he saw her, but she could only stand and stare. He was wearing a black polo-neck sweater with form-fitting black jeans, and he looked so wickedly handsome that her heart turned over.

But she mustn't let him know the effect he had on her.

She made herself walk forward as he came to meet her, and managed a wan smile.

"Hallo, Nick. You frightened me for a minute. I thought I'd forgotten to pay the parking fee."

"Let me have those." He took the shopping-bags from her and carried them to her car. Then he waited while she unlocked the hatchback and stowed them inside.

"I want to talk to you, Sally."

She kept her head lowered, fussing with the shopping. "It's nearly two weeks, Nick."

"I know, and I'm sorry, but – well – it had to be this way."

He reached up and closed the hatchback of the car so she had to turn and face him as he added earnestly, "I've been up to my ears in work. But I'm sure you'll understand when I explain."

She couldn't meet his eyes. "What is there to explain?"

"Everything." He took her hand and held it tenderly between his own. "I'm sorry if I've hurt you, Sally. But – well – there's something I want to show you. Please don't pass judgement on me till you've seen it."

At the touch of his hands, and the appeal in his voice, she knew she could deny him nothing.

"All right," she conceded. "Where is it?"

As his car wasn't there, she assumed that whatever he wanted to show her would be in town, but he said, "A few kilometres away. Gillian's using the Porsche, so we'll have to go in your car. If you don't mind me driving."

She handed him the key in silence.

The Micra was a nippy little car which suited her, but it seemed very small when Nick had folded himself into the driving seat, adjusted to accommodate his long legs. Sally had never ridden as passenger in her own car so she was very conscious of his every move, his hands on the wheel, the tightening of his thigh as his foot pressed on the clutch. She tried to ignore his magnetism and concentrate on where they were going. She couldn't imagine what he would want to show her. Or why.

They drove in silence through open countryside, passed two small hamlets, then he turned in at wrought-iron gates and drew up in front of a lovely old farmhouse, with whitewashed walls and a slate roof so typical of the area.

Sally glanced at Nick. Why had he brought her here?

"Georgian and damp," she muttered, recalling his comment on first seeing her home.

"Georgian and dry. At least, I hope so," he said, climbing out of the car and stretching luxuriously, which made him look so fit and masculine, Sally had to avert her eyes. If she was going to retain her sanity, she must try to forget how intimate they had been.

"I have to give an opinion on this house," he was saying. "You've lived in an old cottage for years, so you know the problems. I'd like you to tell me what you think of the place."

So that was it. Nothing personal. He just wanted to make use of her knowledge.

"I'm not an expert," she said. "You'd do best to employ a surveyor."

"I have." He unlocked the heavy oak door. "It's the day to day things I need to know. How one lives in such a house."

She stepped into the bare hall and the first thing to catch her eye was the staircase.

"It's even finer than the one in our house." She ran her hand over the bannister rail. "It's original, not a copy. You can feel the way it's been worn by polishing."

Nick opened a door. "This is the main room."

He stood just inside, watching her as she gazed around

the unfurnished room, with genuine oak beams in the ceiling, deep-set small-paned windows and –

She moistened her lips and made herself walk across the room to the Delabole slate fireplace which dominated one wall. She stood in front of it, looking down at the black hearth. There was no fire now, but there would have been if the house was occupied.

And suddenly she knew that it wouldn't have mattered. She was no longer afraid.

She turned slowly to face Nick. That night on the moor, he had helped her to overcome her fear. She would always be grateful to him for that, but there was no way she could tell him.

"It's a beautiful fireplace," she said softly.

Something flickered in his eyes, and she hoped he understood. But all he said was, "It's one of the finest I've seen."

He showed her two more rooms on the ground floor, both unfurnished. The one at the back of the house had french windows, which he opened and stepped out onto a paved terrace.

Sally wandered out to look at the garden, a large lawn sloping away from the house, dotted with flowerbeds which were neat but unimaginative. There was a large ornamental cherry tree standing in a carpet of its own pink and gold leaves, and as she gazed at it, her vision blurred and she seemed to be in another garden a long time ago.

"Grandma would love to get her hands on this," she thought, unaware that she had spoken aloud.

"To plant herbs?" Nick asked.

Sally shook her head. "She grows those as a smoke-screen, and because she's interested in folk remedies. There's no point in making a show-place if you want to keep people away." She waved her hand to encompass the view of the sloping lawn and the wooded valley beyond. "We had a beautiful garden at our old home. She could really do something with this."

Nick nodded slowly. "How very interesting."

Something in his tone made Sally suspicious. She glanced sharply at him, then looked up at the house. There were curtains in the windows near the back door – probably the kitchen. And at one of the upstairs windows.

She turned to him, a question in her eyes, but she was sure she already knew the answer.

"This is your house, isn't it?"

Nick studied his fingernails. "I'm sort of camping here at the moment. I needed peace and quiet for my work."

He could have had complete privacy in his suite at The White Hart if he had wanted it. But maybe there was too much gossip for him. She was tempted to ask if he was staying here alone.

She frowned as she saw him surreptitiously consult his watch. Just what was going on? He had brought her here for a purpose. And not to look at the house. Unless he intended to demolish it. Then she heard an unmistakable sound. The slam of a car door. He was expecting someone.

There was the click of high-heels on the path, then Gillian appeared round the side of the house. Very chic, in a black suit, she was escorting an elegant elderly woman in a stylish navy coat, her softly-curled white hair framing her face.

Sally thought it might be Nick's mother. Then her mouth dropped open in astonishment.

"Grandma!"

Mrs Penrose hesitated, but Gillian held her arm and brought her out to the centre of the terrace.

Sally couldn't take her eyes off her grandmother. For seven years she had hidden at home, afraid to show her face. And she never looked into a mirror. But she must have used one today. Instead of being drawn back into a bun, her hair had been cut and curled. And her face was so skilfully made-up, there was no sign of the scars, the disfigurement which had blighted her life.

"Grandma, you look lovely," she breathed.

Her grandmother kissed Sally's cheek. "That's an exaggeration, dear. But thank you."

Sally glanced at Gillian, at Nick, and back to her grandmother. "But how? I mean –"

Nick smiled. "It's all my fault."

"Most things are," Gillian said, her lovely amber eyes bright with enthusiasm. "It's my job, Sally. I'm a beautician. When Nick told me about your grandma, I knew I just had to try to help her."

Mrs Penrose said apologetically, "Gillian came while you were at the market last week, Sally. It *was* Nick's car you saw, but he wasn't driving."

Sally said uncertainly, "There seems to have been some sort of conspiracy –"

"Not really dear. When Gillian told me what she could do, I was – well –" She glanced at Gillian. "Rather sceptical. I didn't want to tell you until I was sure."

Sally was hurt that her grandmother hadn't confided in her. "I see," she said stiffly.

"No, dear, you don't see. That's the trouble. And neither did I." She put her fingers nervously to her cheek. "For years I've never looked in a mirror. I didn't want to see those hideous red and purple scars. But they've faded, Sally. And I never knew."

She pulled off her glove and gazed at the white marks on the back of her hand.

"Gillian thrust a mirror in front of me and made me look. With clever make-up, they hardly show at all."

"They *don't* show at all," Gillian put in firmly.

Mrs Penrose took Sally's hand. "All these years, Sally, I've tied you to the house."

"Never!" Sally said fiercely. "You saved my life, Grandma. I owe it to you."

"But not like this." She glanced at Nick. "It wasn't until Nick came onto the scene that I realised how restricted your life has been."

Gillian smiled. "Your fault again, Nick."

He said wryly, "It always is."

Mrs Penrose gazed around in wonder. "Here I am, miles away from home. Yet only a few weeks ago I was wondering if I would ever go out again. And it's all thanks to you, Gillian."

"You're forgetting your own courage, my dear." She took Mrs Penrose by the arm. "It's been rather traumatic for you. Let's go and find a cup of coffee."

"I do feel a bit overwhelmed." Mrs Penrose let herself be led away.

Sally too was overwhelmed. Her grandmother had been restored to the attractive woman she used to be. Had she been blind all these years? Could her grandmother have returned to normal life long before this?

Racked with doubt and uncertainty, she needed to lash out at something. She turned abruptly to Nick.

"Why did you bring Grandma to your love-nest!"

He blinked in surprise. "What do you mean?"

"Well," she accused. "Gillian's staying here with you, isn't she!"

"Yes, but –"

"And she's your mistress."

His eyebrows shot up. "Don't be ridiculous. She's my sister."

Sally snorted. "You expect me to believe that! You only

have to look at her. She's not a bit like you. Amber eyes and auburn hair. And that's not dyed," she added emphatically.

"No. It's the colour of her father's hair. But Sally –"

"And her name. Masters, because she's married. But when we were talking about folklore at the dance –" Sally pointed accusingly. "She called *you* Dewer. It wasn't her name."

"No, her name was Scott. She's my half-sister."

Sally sniffed in disgust, but he went on, "I told you my father walked out when I was two. My mother married again a few years later. Gillian looks like her father, I look like mine."

Sally wasn't wholly convinced. "She was sharing your suite at The White Hart. Everybody says she's your mistress."

Nick smote his brow in horror. "My God! The poor girl. After all she's been through."

He strode agitatedly along the terrace and back again. "And you believed it?"

Sally nodded.

"No wonder you called me the Devil."

He closed his eyes for a moment, drawing in a deep breath. "It's not the sort of thing I'd tell anyone, but I guess you'd better know. Gillian's recently been through a rather messy divorce."

He waved his hand dismissively. "No need to go into details, but she was on the verge of a nervous breakdown. She went to St John's Wood to recouperate."

He sighed. "Some hope! Mother is – to say the least – unsympathetic. She likes to organise everyone, and she was driving Gillian up the wall. That's why I brought her here with me, to give her a chance to find her feet again."

He shook his head slowly. "I told them at the hotel she's my sister. It never occurred to me that anyone would think otherwise. The poor girl...."

Sally didn't know what to say. She remembered at the dance Jake had said Gillian was Nick's sister, but the others had poured scorn on it. And she had believed them.

Nick said thoughtfully, "Gillian must've heard the gossip, but it doesn't seem to have bothered her. She told me only yesterday how she loves this part of the country."

"Perhaps she's found her feet again," Sally suggested.

Nick nodded. "You're probably right. Don't be surprised if you see a beauty parlour opening up soon."

"She's very good," Sally said. "She's bound to be a success. Look what she's done for Grandma...."

Her words trailed away and she turned to gaze across the garden, not really seeing any of it. Grandma was free to lead her own life now. She would probably give up the bees, they weren't needed for protection any more. She might pick up with some of her old friends again, though she was more likely to take an active role in the life of the town, especially the campaign to save The Duke's.

Gillian's life had been sorted out too. She would start a new enterprise. Nick seemed interested in this house, and he had all his building projects.

But what about herself? Her whole life had been turned upside down. What was she going to do now....

Nick said softly, "I want to show you something, Sally."

She turned uncertain blue eyes upon him. "But I've seen Grandma. That's why you brought me here, isn't it? Somewhere secure for Grandma to make her first venture from home."

"That was Gillian's idea. I want to show you what I've been working on."

Sally was suddenly alert. His most pressing problem was how to get permission to demolish The Duke's. He must have been working on that. Though she was surprised that he wanted to show her what he was doing.

"Plans for the town?" she asked warily.

"The new supermarket." He turned towards the french windows. "This way."

Sally followed him sceptically. Was this another ploy? Taking advantage of her confusion over seeing her grandmother's transformation.

"You won't make me give in. I'll fight to the last to save our theatre."

He took her to a large room at the far end of the house, and she could see what he meant about camping here. The room was bare except for a wooden chair, two tables and a drawing board, all littered with drawings, set-squares, sheets of paper, pencils, rulers....

Nick closed the door and strode across to the drawing-board. "Can you understand architects' drawings?"

"I expect so." She watched him cautiously. "But I don't want to see how you intend to ruin our town."

"It won't be ruined." He stood aside and held out his hand. "Come and have a look."

Sally shrugged. Since she was here, she might as well see what they were up against. She walked over to the drawing-board and scanned the drawing.

"You've put out the wrong one."

"What makes you think that?"

"This is the 'Before' drawing." She pointed. "It shows The Duke's."

"So?"

She lifted her chin. "What do you mean, so! You know you can't build your rotten supermarket while that's there."

He looked down at the drawing. "I've discovered that I can."

Sally blinked in disbelief. "You can?"

He kept his eyes on the drawing. "It's tricky, and it's taken a hell of a lot of work. But by going up instead of out, widening the access and making maximum use of the carpark, I should just be able to fit it all in."

"And leave The Duke's intact?" she breathed.

He nodded. "It should be possible."

She gazed at him in wonder. Had he really changed his mind? "But why? You've always been so adamant. Calling it a heap of old stones."

"So it is. In an appalling state of repair."

She ran her fingers through her hair in bewilderment. "Then what –? I don't understand."

'Neither did I, at first. That's what made things so confusing." He caught hold of her shoulders and pulled her round to face him. "Sally Penrose, you've turned my life inside out."

"I have?"

"You, and your grandmother, and your friends." He sighed. "I came to this town to do a nice simple job. Demolish some old buildings and put up a spanking new supermarket. But I ran straight into opposition from an unexpected quarter. Young people steeped in tradition and folklore, who wanted to save a grotty old building, which to my mind should have been condemned years ago."

He smiled. "But you taught me that there's more to life than efficiency. There's sentiment and a love of history. And how can logic fight those? You and your friends love that old theatre. Who am I to say you are wrong?"

Her eyes lit up with joy. "Oh Nick. Do you really mean it? The battle's over? The Duke's won't have to come down?"

"It'll fall down if restoration work isn't started immediately."

"Oh." Her spirits sank. She knew it would be expensive and the campaign didn't have any money.

Nick looked down at the drawing and ran his finger round the outline of The Duke's Theatre. He said softly, "You win, Sally Penrose. I'll submit this new plan, and I'll undertake the restoration. On one condition."

Sally was getting bemused with all these unexpected turns, and the ominous tone of his voice quelled her rising elation.

"What's that?"

"On condition that you marry me."

For one second she thought she had gone stark raving mad. She must be having hallucinations. He couldn't possibly....

"Marry you?" she stammered.

He nodded. "That's what I said."

Marry him! Sally gazed towards the window, her heart soaring with happiness as a rosy picture filled her mind. To live with him in this lovely old house – she was sure now that it was his – to see him every day, to spend every night in his arms....

Then her eye fell upon the drawing. The new plan that would save the theatre. But at what a price! All that talk about sentiment! He hadn't changed at all. He didn't love her, he wanted to buy her.

"No!"

He took her hand, his dark eyes searching her face. "But Sally, I thought –"

"It's a mean underhand trick. I won't sell myself for the theatre!" She tried to snatch her hand away.

But he held it firmly. "I'm not asking you to. I'm going to submit that plan anyway." He lifted her hand to his lips. "That was just a rather clumsy lead in. I'm asking you to marry me."

He hadn't said that he loved her. "You don't believe in marriage."

"No. Until now, I never have." He pressed her hand to his lips again. "You turned my life upside down, Sally."

As you did mine, she thought, the touch of his lips making her pulse begin to race.

"The moment I saw you on stage, I wanted you." His gaze moved slowly over her. "I'll admit it was purely physical. You're so lovely. And at first you responded so readily."

He drew her towards him and she was powerless to resist.

"But you kept losing your temper and you had me all confused." His lips brushed her forehead. "I thought you were only playing innocent to keep me dangling on a string. But that night on the moor, when I held you in my arms, I knew I wanted to hold you and protect you for ever."

"That was a fortnight ago," she said, still pained by his long silence. "You could have contacted me."

"I wouldn't have known what to say, Sally. I was completely thrown. I've never felt like that about any woman before."

He waved his hand towards the drawing-board. "That's why I came here. I needed time to think, to sort out my emotions." He smiled. "And to work out a new plan."

"Why?" she asked softly. "Why have you decided to save the theatre?"

He looked down into her eyes, and her heart turned over. "Because I love you, Sally. With all my heart, my mind, and my intellect. And I'll do anything to make you happy."

"You love me?" she whispered. "Oh Nick."

He bent his head and his lips met hers in a kiss of infinite tenderness, which told her more than words could say.

His voice was husky as he asked, "You *will* marry me, Sally?"

She slid her arms round his neck. "Not for the theatre, Nick. But because I love you."

"Oh Sally." He crushed her to him and she responded with all the love in her heart.

As she nestled happily against his chest, she caught sight of two drawings pinned on the wall. She was surprised that he had kept them, the Devil caricatures she had put on her placards.

"Dewer the Devil," she mused. "I've just realised, Nick. When I marry you, I'll be Mrs Devil."

"And all our children will be little Devils."

She smiled. "If they're anything like you, they're bound to be."

"Ah, but if they're like you, they'll be angels," he murmured as his lips met hers again.